MAINE MEN
TWO TALES

K.C. WELLS

A New Path (A Maine Men story)

Cover Art by Meredith Russell
Watercolour illustration by Alexandra Kalenova
(Shutterstock.com)

Follow Your Heart (A Maine Men story)

Cover Art by Meredith Russell
Artist: Dan Skinner

ISBN: 978-1-916853-73-7

Warning

This book contains material that is intended for a mature, adult audience. It contains graphic language, explicit sexual content, and adult situations.

A New PATH
A Maine Men STORY
K.C. WELLS

Part One

Joel came out of the bathroom to be greeted by the aromas of freshly brewed coffee, and bacon. He let out a contented sigh. "You spoil me."

Finn chuckled. "You deserve it, Mr. Financial Wizard. You've worked damn hard this week. All *I* did was a lot of hammering and swearing." The hotel was up, and all work now centered on the interior. Joel had suggested staying in one of the ocean front suites when it finally opened, and Finn's eyes had got that wicked gleam in them that Joel loved so much.

Joel sauntered over to where Finn was pouring him a cup of coffee, and snaked his arms around Finn's waist, pressing his still damp chest to Finn's back. "Where's Bramble?"

Finn inclined his head toward the back door. "Sniffing around out in the yard. I swore I caught sight of a little rabbit out there first thing this morning. Maybe Bramble can smell it."

Joel hoped to God the rabbit was long gone. He leaned in and whispered, "Do we have time?"

Finn laughed. "You are *such* a horn dog. You got a blow job when you woke up, didn't you?"

Joel let the towel around his hips fall to the ground, then ground his dick against Finn's jeans-encased ass. "He wants in."

Finn dropped his head to Joel's shoulder with a shiver. "And I want him in, but… bacon."

"It can keep warm, can't it?"

Finn reached back to curl his fingers around Joel's hard cock, and groaned. "Damn, you feel good."

Joel's phone vibrated on the kitchen table, and Joel sighed. "Hold that thought." He picked up his towel, secured it, and picked up the phone. "It's Nate." He tapped *Answer.* "Hey, buddy. You're up early for a Saturday."

"Hey, Dad. Are you and Finn home today?"

"Yup. We're just about to… have breakfast."

Finn smothered a chuckle.

"Would it be okay if I came over?"

Joel stilled. "Sure, but—"

"I know I'll be seeing you next weekend for my birthday but… I really need to talk to you, and I don't want to do that when the house will be full with Mom, Laura, Eric, Aunt Megan and Aunt Lynne…"

The anxious edge to Nate's voice only left one course of action.

"Come over for lunch. Although I warn

you, it'll be meat. Finn got us a grill, and he's been waiting all week to try it out."

"Sounds great. I'll see you then." Nate disconnected the call.

Joel put the phone down on the kitchen table.

"Sweetheart? What is it?"

Joel met Finn's troubled gaze. "Nate's coming, and there's something wrong. I can feel it."

Finn took Joel in his arms. "Okay… worrying about it isn't gonna change a thing. That's just a waste of energy. So here's what we're gonna do. We'll eat breakfast. I'll take care of lunch—*you* make sure the place is presentable. Not that it ever gets all *that* messy." He smiled. "My boyfriend is neat."

"And what about…?" Joel lowered his gaze to his crotch.

Finn cupped Joel's bulge. "He can wait." Then he gave Joel a sweet kiss on the lips. "Nate's more important right now."

Joel looped his arms around Finn's neck. "Have I told you lately how much I love you?"

Finn smiled. "Maybe? But tell me again anyway."

Joel looked into gunmetal eyes. "I love you."

Finn closed the gap between them and kissed him, a lingering, promising kiss. "Love you too. Now go put some clothes on, you walking wet dream." Joel preened, and he laughed. "Clothes. Now."

Joel released him and headed for the stairs to the loft bedroom.

What's going on, Nate?

He'd find out soon enough.

Nate turned off the engine and sagged into the seat. *This is so messed up.* He'd avoided Mom's calls all week: he should have known her intuition would kick in. *I'm not ready to say anything yet.* He wasn't sure he was ready to tell Dad, but he had to talk to *someone* before he exploded.

He got out of the car. Before he reached the front porch, Finn was at the side gate, waving at him.

"We're back here." He glanced to the side. "Bramble, will you just wait?"

Nate took the path around to the side of the house, and no sooner was he through the gate than Bramble was leaping up to be petted. Nate stroked his silky ears. "How's my favorite dog?"

Finn gave him a hug. "Hey. Good to see you. Your dad's tinkering with the grill."

Nate widened his eyes. "You let him near it? What were you thinking?" They both laughed.

Nate followed Finn into the backyard, Bramble trotting ahead of them, to where his dad was standing at the grill, scowling.

"Is this hot enough yet?"

Nate peered at the coals. "No. And you've spread them too soon. Leave the coals in a heap until they've got gray ash all over them. That means they're smoldering all the way through."

Joel arched his eyebrows. "Do they teach you how to grill in college?"

Nate managed a chuckle. "No, Dad. Eric's ace at grilling."

"Are you saying I'm not?" Joel held up his hand. "Wait. Don't answer that."

Despite his roiling stomach, Nate grinned.

"Am I missing something?" Finn demanded.

"Well…"

Joel fired him a warning look. "Don't. He does *not* need to hear that."

Nate bit his lip. "All I'm gonna say is… Finn? *You* do the grilling."

Finn strolled over to his dad, and kissed him. "Aw. It's okay, honey. Your gifts lie in… other directions." Nate was trying hard not to react.

"He's talking about my lasagna," Joel protested.

"Sure. We'll go with that." Finn's eyes twinkled.

Nate loved seeing his dad and Finn together. They just… fit.

"Want a soda?" Finn asked. "Or a coffee?"

"Water would be good."

Finn went up the steps onto the deck and into the house.

Joel held his arms wide. "Do I get a hug?"

Nate didn't hesitate. He stepped into the circle of his dad's arms and hugged him tightly. Then Joel released him and pointed to the patio couch on the deck.

"We can sit out here if you like. It's not *that* cold."

Nate followed him up the steps, and they sat on the comfortable couch. He leaned against the cushions, his heartbeat racing. Right on cue, Bramble sat in front of him, his nose resting on Nate's knee. "Good boy," he said quietly, stroking Bramble's soft coat.

Finn returned with three bottles of water, and handed him one. Then he pulled up one of the armchairs and sat in that.

"Your call had me worried," Joel said in a low voice. "You sounded… I don't know… anxious."

"I've got stuff on my mind, that's all." And it had been on his mind for way too long.

"Stuff you can share?"

Nate bit his lip.

"How's school?" Finn asked. "Now that

you're not living at home anymore."

"My roommates are cool. They're all guys I met in different classes last semester, and we get along great." He snorted. "Well, *most* of the time." Dean and Mike could be real dicks sometimes, Dean especially.

"That's good." Joel took a drink from his bottle. "I remember there were a couple of assholes when I was a sophomore. It's good if you're all friends."

He'd waited long enough. "I read what you wrote about when you were younger… but… did you *really* know you were gay in elementary school?"

Joel blinked. "I had an inkling. And as I got older, that feeling just… grew."

Nate nodded. "And the way you felt about boys… you never felt that way about girls?"

Joel shook his head. "Where are you going with all this?"

Tell him. Just tell *him.*

"I like girls," he began.

Joel grinned. "We know that. All you did this summer was talk about some girl in your class. Mia, is that her name?"

Nate's cheeks grew hot. "Did I talk about her a lot?"

Finn chuckled. "Oh, not much. Just every time you were here, that's all."

Nate's heart pounded. "The thing is… I

kinda talked about her because that was way easier than saying what was really on my mind." His pulse quickened. "You see… there are lots of girls—*and* guys—I think are really cool. And I never really thought anything about that—until this summer."

"What happened? And is there one guy in particular?" Joel's voice was soft.

Nate expelled a breath. "How did you know this is to do with a guy?"

"Call it intuition." Joel smiled. "You're here, talking to two gay men. Duh."

Relief washed over him. *This is going to be okay.*

"So what's his name?" Finn asked.

"Carter… he's one of my roommates… and…" He swallowed. "I can't stop thinking about him. I mean, all the freakin' time. So… does that mean I'm gay? Bi? Pan?"

Because right now I have no fucking clue.

Joel's eyes widened, and his breath caught. Finn leaned forward. "How about we leave the labels to one side for a minute?"

Nate could go with that. Labels were confusing the hell out of him.

"First of all, Mia… have you and she dated?"

"Yeah, for a while—then she dumped me. I think she was actually more interested in my roommate, Dean."

"Okay." Finn sat back. "This roommate of

yours, Carter… tell me about him."

Nate drew in a deep breath. "He's my best friend. We met the first week of freshman year. So when he said they were looking for a fourth guy to share a suite, I said yes. I knew the others." He shivered. "What I hadn't counted on was the effect spending more time around him would have on me."

"How long have you had feelings for him?" Joel asked.

Nate stared at him. "You're okay with this, aren't you?"

Joel's eyes glistened. "Tell me you haven't been worrying about how I'd react. With *my* history? What did you think I'd do—say 'No, no, no, you're straight?'"

"I didn't know *what* I was thinking, to be honest. My head's been such a mess for months now." Nate took another calming breath. "I guess I started thinking… that way… about him this summer. We met up a lot. He was teaching me how to surf."

Joel stared at him. "Does your mom know about him? She never mentioned you'd been surfing."

"That's because I didn't tell her." Another slow tide of heat crawled up his neck. "I couldn't. She'd have asked too many questions, and I wasn't ready to tell her."

"Why? You have to know she wouldn't

react badly."

Nate struggled to frame his thoughts. "After seeing how Mom and Laura were fine with you and Finn being together, I knew they wouldn't have a problem with it. *I* was the one with the problem." He rolled the bottle between his palms. "I guess it threw me. I'd never thought about a guy… like that, and it just confused the hell out of me."

"There's this great word that sums up how you're feeling." Finn smiled. "Discombobulated."

Nate chuckled. "Okay, that's a really neat word. It even sounds right."

"Is he good looking?" Finn asked.

Nate said nothing, but pulled his phone from his pocket. He opened the gallery and scrolled. He held out the phone to Finn. "This was taken last week. We went for a hike in Acadia, and I took a selfie. He pulled goofy faces, so I did too."

Finn peered at the screen, then glanced at Joel. "Nate has good taste."

Joel smiled. "Like his dad." He leaned over to look. He studied the image for a moment. "I guess this is the point where I ask if he's into guys."

Nate stared at Carter. "I don't know. And that's the part that's killing me.
What if this is all one-sided? Do I say nothing, or… do I tell him how I feel?" He raised his head and gazed at them. "And if I do say something, what if this all goes to shit, and I ruin everything?"

"You'd do that? Tell him, I mean?" Finn gaped. "You are one brave dude."

"You think I shouldn't?" There were moments when Nate was absolutely convinced it was the right thing to do, and others when he thought he'd be crazy to even contemplate such a move.

"We can't advise you on that," Joel said in a low voice. "Yes, it could all go sideways, but you need to decide if that's the chance you're prepared to take." He sighed. "Whichever path you choose, we're here for you, okay? Whether that's to congratulate you on finding him, support you in your decision not to tell him how you feel—or give you a hug because it didn't work out. If it's the latter, that comes with pizza, popcorn, and sitting through any movies of your choice." His eyes gleamed. "Which is pretty brave of me, knowing your taste in movies."

Nate laughed. Finally getting the words out lifted his spirits a little. It didn't bring him any closer to knowing what he was going to do next—if anything—but at least he knew Joel and Finn had his back.

His stomach rumbled, and he gave them a sheepish glance. "When's lunch?"

Finn laughed. "And that's my cue to go fetch the meat. The potato salad is already made in the fridge—and it's your mom's recipe."

Joel held out his arm again, and Nate

shifted closer for a hug. "Don't think about it now. Just eat, and enjoy the peace and quiet—and Bramble fussing to go on a W-A-L-K." Bramble's ears pricked up, and Joel groaned. "Yup, it's official. My dog can spell."

"And you can stay as long as you like," Finn added. "There's always a futon here with your name on it, you know that."

"Thanks, Finn, Dad." This was exactly what he needed—a little breathing space, some time away from Carter to think, to decide…

To plan his next move—if there was going to be one.

Part Two

Nate walked into the living room, where Dean, Mike, and Carter were sprawled on the couch, watching the game.

Dean glanced in his direction. "Hey. Wanna join us? There's still some popcorn left. That's if Mike hasn't hogged it all."

"Fuck you," Mike said good-naturedly. "And there's plenty more where that came from."

"Thanks, but I'm gonna go to my room." Nate wrinkled his nose at the pizza boxes lying open on the coffee table, still with the odd slice of pizza congealing in them. "Whose turn is it to clean up?"

"You tell me, Mr. Roster Man," Mike quipped. "You're the neat freak around here."

Carter hit him on the arm. "Stop that. And Nate had the right idea, drawing up a chore chart." He winked at Nate. "We need *someone* around here who isn't a slob. I'll make sure they clean up after themselves."

"Thanks." Nate walked into the kitchen, grabbed a can of soda from the fridge, and escaped to the sanctuary of his room. No way could he sit with them, not when Carter was wearing his tank top that revealed his tanned chest and the slight curve of his biceps. And those shorts…

I think he'd notice if I started drooling all over the rug.

Nate sat on his bed, stuffed pillows behind him, and picked up his laptop. He needed to read through his essay before Monday, and if it was a choice between working or being tortured by the sight of Carter, he'd settle for work any day.

There was a quiet knock at his door.

"Come in."

It opened, and Carter stuck his head around it. "You got a minute?"

Nate's heart went into overdrive. "Sure." Disconcertingly, the word came out as a squeak.

Carter came into the room and closed the door behind him, just as Dean and Mike started whooping and hollering. Carter chuckled. "I guess someone scored." He peered at the laptop. "If you're busy, I can come back later."

Nate closed it and placed it to one side. "No, I'm not busy. What's up?"

Carter sat at the foot of the bed. "Well, first of all, I wanted to know if you'd like to go for a hike in Acadia tomorrow. If I asked those guys, I think we both know what the answer would be."

Nate laughed. "In the dictionary under 'couch potato', it says 'See them'. And sure. You got a particular hike in mind?"

"There's the Ocean Path trail. It goes along

the coast. And the forecast isn't too bad." Carter smiled. "I just need to get the wind through my hair, blow away a few cobwebs, that's all."

"Sounds great. What time would we have to leave?"

"First thing in the morning. It'll take a couple of hours to get there." Carter grinned. "Don't worry, I'll bang on your door till I know you're awake. And if that doesn't work, I'll come in, yank the comforter back, and pour cold water on you."

Nate gaped. "Don't even think about it." Then he recalled Carter's words. "You said first of all. Is there something else?"

Carter drew his long legs up onto the bed and crossed them at the ankles, and Nate quickly averted his gaze when he realized he was checking out Carter's crotch.

Carter leaned back on his hands. "How was your dad? And what's his boyfriend's name? Finn?"

Nate nodded. "They're fine. It was good to see them." Carter fell silent, and Nate's scalp prickled. "That's it? You just wanted to ask how my dad is doing?"

Carter tilted his head to one side. "Does it feel weird? Seeing him with a guy, I mean."

Nate smiled. "Not at all. Okay, it was a shock when I first found out Dad was gay. But I already liked Finn, and you only have to see them together to know they're perfect for each other." He hesitated. "When I think back on how Dad and Mom used to be with each other… They didn't argue, but… They were never a couple who hugged and kissed a lot, you know?"

"And do your dad and Finn kiss a lot?"

Nate's face grew hot. "God, yeah. Sometimes I get the feeling when I'm around them that if I just went to the bathroom, they'd be all over each other." He narrowed his gaze. "That doesn't gross you out, does it?"

Carter smiled. "Love is love, right?"

Nate blinked. "That's what I think too."

Carter nodded. "It sounds like your dad is happy finally being his true self. All power to him."

"That was kinda deep." Nate arched his eyebrows.

Carter chuckled. "Hey, I just tell it like I see it." He got up from the bed. "We can do a hike every weekend if you like, till the weather closes in."

"Sounds good, except not next weekend."

"You got plans?"

Nate chuckled. "Well, my parents do. It's my birthday this week, so we're all going to my dad's on Saturday. And my Aunt Megan and her partner Lynne are coming too."

Carter stared. "Wow. Is there an LGBTQ+ gene in your family?"

Nate's heart hammered. "Maybe?"

Carter nodded toward Nate's laptop. "I'll let you get back to work."

As he reached the door, Nate called out, "Looking forward to this hike tomorrow."

Carter turned and smiled. "Me too." Then he was gone.

Nate stared at the white painted door. A walk with Carter…

He wasn't sure whether that would be heaven—or hell.

They headed for a gap in the trees, and emerged onto a rocky bluff of warm, beige-and-gold stone. Below them, the ocean pounded the shore, waves crashing over rocks to form pools. Trees sprang up between the clefts in the rock, spreading their branches out over the edge.

"This is great." Nate inhaled deeply, drawing the ocean air into his lungs. "Do you come here often?"

Carter chuckled. "That sounds like a really bad pick-up line. And yeah, this is one of my fave spots." He clambered onto a broad, flat rock and drew his knees up. "Snack time."

Nate laughed. "You brought snacks? All I brought was water. You should've told me."

"Why? I've got enough for you too."

Carter pulled two sandwiches from his backpack, both covered in wrap, and held one out to Nate. "Tuna. I know you like that."

Nate took it with a smile. "Yeah. Thanks. That's one of *my* faves." He grinned. "Next to my mom's meatloaf sandwiches."

Carter rolled his eyes. "And now I want a meatloaf sandwich. I can't tell you the last time I had a really good one." He unwrapped the wedge of bread, its filling almost as thick.

Nate chuckled. "I feel as if I need to be one of those snakes that can unhinge their jaws to get this in my mouth."

"Hey, when it comes to sandwiches, I don't mess around." Carter took a bite and stared out at the ocean.

Nate ate, and the silence between them felt comfortable. Not that it was really silence: the crashing waves and shrieks of gulls saw to that. He paused between bites. "This is really good."

"I made them this morning, before I woke you up."

"Yeah, about that." Nate narrowed his gaze. "Did you *have* to tickle my feet?"

Carter widened his eyes. "It worked, didn't it?"

Nate stared at him for a moment, then burst into laughter. He couldn't remember the last time he'd felt so… content. Relaxed. At peace with himself. His inner turmoil of the previous day had melted into nothingness, and a lot of that was down to Carter.

He doesn't do stress. Carter exuded the laidback charm of a surfer dude, with his tangle of unruly blond curls and tanned face and neck.

"I think you're good for me," Nate announced between bites.

"Oh yeah? How?"

"I was getting stressed out about… something, and this has helped."

Carter smiled. "That's why I come here. It's a good place to leave the real world behind, and think about other stuff."

"What kind of stuff do you think about?" Nate stilled. "Sorry, you don't have to answer that. It's none of my beeswax anyhow."

Carter grinned. "Beeswax. My Aunt Charlotte says that a lot."

"I picked it up from Finn. God knows where he got it from." Nate chuckled. "He says it a lot too."

"You like him, don't you?"

Nate nodded. "He's really cool. He's in construction. Dad says Finn is going to build them a house one day. Someplace along the coast where they can see the ocean."

"That sounds great."

"Yeah, it is."

Carter took another bite. "I don't mind telling you what I think about. In fact, I've been meaning to share that for a while now. I just never got up enough nerve. Maybe that's why I asked you to come. It's not the sort of thing I could say back at the house."

Nate arched his eyebrows. "Why not?"

Carter bit his lip. "Because I wouldn't want Dean or Mike walking in on us while we were talking."

Nate swallowed. "Whatever it is you've been thinking about… is it important?"

Carter gave a slow nod, his gaze focused on Nate.

When nothing else was forthcoming, Nate took a drink from his bottle of water, his throat a little tight. "Okay then. Wanna tell me what's been on your mind?"

Carter said nothing for a moment, then lowered his gaze. "Now I'm here, it's not so easy." He glanced at Nate. "You ever have times where you know what you want to say, you plan it all out in your head, but when the right time comes along, you freeze?"

Nate laughed quietly. "Hoo yeah." He understood that all too well.

Carter sighed. "I've wanted to say this for a while, but I wasn't sure how you'd react."

Nate stilled. "This sounds kinda serious."

Carter held up his hand. "Can you let me get this out, please? Now that I'm finally at this point, I don't want to stop." Nate nodded, and mimed zipping his lips, and Carter expelled a breath. "Okay. I asked how you felt about your dad and his boyfriend, because I wasn't sure if you were okay with that. I think you spent most of the last year pissed. Then when I saw how you accepted them… well, it helped me come to a decision." Carter lowered his gaze. "I figured if you were okay with your dad being gay, then you'd be okay with… me being gay."

Nate forgot how to breathe.

Carter jerked his head up. "Is it that much of a shock?"

"No," Nate protested. "You just surprised me, is all." That had to be the understatement of the year. Carter had blindsided him with his declaration.

"And you're okay with it?" Carter swallowed.

"Of course I am, but why should it matter if I'm okay with it?"

Carter's gaze met his. "Because the last thing I wanted to do was lose my best friend." He smiled. "Which is you, in case you missed that part."

Nate forced a smile. "That's cool." His stomach clenched. No way was he about to reveal his feelings, not after that. It would feel… presumptuous. *Gee, that's great, Carter. By the way, I think I'm in love with you.*

Yeah no.

His chest tightened. Carter had been upfront with him, and he was still hiding.

"You were right about me being pissed, by the way," he murmured. "I was so angry with my dad. I mean, I thought he'd abandoned my mom, betrayed her—and me and Laura too. Then when I learned the truth…" He took a deep breath. "The thing is… finding out he was gay just added to the mind-fuck I was living through."

Carter's brow furrowed. "What? You never said anything."

"I couldn't, okay? And to be honest, it was so… I'm not sure if the word I'm searching for is coincidental or ironic. You see, there was my dad, telling us he liked guys, had *always* liked guys, and there was me… discovering that…" Nate seized his courage with both hands and held on tight. "That I like girls… *and* guys."

Carter stared at him. "Oh wow." Then he grinned. "Today seems to be the day for confessions, doesn't it?" He cocked his head. "Does Mia know? That… that wasn't why she dumped you, was it? Because she found out you're bi?"

Nate shook his head. "She dumped me for a new flavor, that's all. And no, she doesn't know. The only people who do, are my dad, Finn… and you."

Carter flushed. "I'm honored." His eyes sparkled. "It feels good to get it out, doesn't it?"

He whooshed out a breath. "Man, I've been bottling that up for so long."

Nate chuckled, overwhelmed by the feeling of lightness that spread through him. "I know what you mean." His mouth had suddenly dried up, and he took a drink from his bottle. He was dying to ask if Carter was interested in anyone, but he didn't dare.

I might not like the answer.

Carter leaned back on his hands, his knees bent, gazing at the ocean. "So… is there someone you're thinking of asking out?"

Yes, and it's you.

Nate wasn't *that* brave. "No. How about you? Any guys on your radar?"

Please say no. Please say no. Please say no.

"Well… there might be."

Aw fuck.

Nate pasted on a smile. "Wow. That's pretty epic. I hope it works out for you."

Tell him. Let him know you're interested.

Nope. It still felt pretty presumptuous. *Hey, Carter, this guy you're interested in… I think you should forget about him, because you'd be better off with me.*

Yeah. *So* not happening.

Carter drained the last of his water. "I'm glad we talked. And about Dean and Mike… I'm not ready for them to know just yet. So can we keep this between us?"

"Sure. As long as you keep my secret too."

Carter's smile reached his eyes. "It's safe with me." He got to his feet. "Come on. We've got some hiking to do." Then he stilled. "Thank you. I was really nervous about coming out with all that." He chuckled. "Look what I did."

"I guess we both came out." Nate hoped he was doing the right thing staying silent. It had obviously been a huge deal for Carter: Nate didn't want to complicate the situation even further.

Not yet. When the time is right.

Nate prayed he would recognize the right time when it came along.

PART THREE

Nate leaned back in his chair and stretched. The essay was as good as he could make it. There were times when he wondered how Dean and Mike expected to pass any exams—they seemed to spend all their time on their phones, watching movies, and drinking.

His phone buzzed, and he glanced at the screen. It was a text from Mom.

Got a minute?

He clicked *Call*. "Hey. What's up?"

"I'm calling about Saturday. And to wish you a happy birthday for tomorrow."

He chuckled. "You know, you could always call me tomorrow to do that?"

"I know, but you'll have classes, so I wanted to get it in early. Are you going to do anything nice for your birthday?"

"Nope. I've got classes all day. I'll save my celebrating for Saturday."

"About that… You can bring a guest, you know. If there's someone you'd like to invite along."

Nate saw right through that, but he wasn't about to let his mom know. "I'll see."

"Okay. One last thing, because it's late. Do

you want to go to your dad's with me, Eric, and Laura in my car? Or do you want to meet us there?"

"I'm not sure. Can I let you know?"

She chuckled. "As long as you give me plenty of notice. Enjoy tomorrow if you can."

"Thanks, Mom. See you Saturday." He disconnected, smiling to himself. *She wants to know if I'm seeing anyone.* Mom had met Mia in the summer. He'd brought her to a family barbecue, and his dad and Finn had come over too. Nate got the impression his dad had been curious about Eric, and vice versa. It could have been weird, his parents introducing their respective partners for the first time, but Eric and Joel hit it off.

Ask Carter.

Nate shoved that thought aside instantly. Why would Carter agree to come?

It had been three days since their hike, and Nate hadn't seen much of him. And in those three days, Nate had started to have second thoughts.

I should have told him how I felt. Nate knew what had stopped him—those three little words when he'd asked Carter if there was someone.

There might be.

But *might* implied some element of doubt. What if he waited too long, and Carter's *might* became a reality?

Either he's interested in me, or he's not. If it was the latter, sure, that would sting, but it was better to know, right? And if he wasn't, then Nate could move on and find someone who was.

Except he didn't want anyone else. He wanted Carter.

All this thinking was getting him nowhere. And now he needed to pee.

Nate got up from his chair and went to the door. The house was quiet, which meant Dean and Mike were out: silent was not in their vocabulary. He headed for the bathroom. Whoever had built suites with only one bath had obviously never anticipated students. Fights for the bathroom took on epic proportions at times.

He relieved himself, flushed, then washed his hands. As he stepped back into the hallway, the door facing him opened, and Carter stuck his head out. "Hey. I was just thinking about you."

Nate stared at him. "Oh my God, what did you do?" Carter's tangled mass of blond curls was gone, replaced by a sleek, short cut that Nate had to admit was damn sexy.

"I got it done this morning. I was tired of looking like a slob, so I told him to chop it all off." Carter frowned. "Don't you like it?"

Nate hoped to God Carter didn't look down, because then he would know *exactly* how much Nate liked it—his sweats did a terrible job of hiding his boner. "I do like it, honest. It was just such a… surprise, that's all."

Carter inclined his head toward his room.

"I was just looking up some new hikes for us. Wanna see?"

"Sure." He followed Carter into the room. Carter's laptop was open on the bed, and there was a map displayed.

"I need to know how adventurous you're prepared to be," Carter said as he sat on the bed. "Because there's this one hike that's a hell of a climb, but I think it would be awesome."

"Show me." Nate sat on the opposite side of the bed and peered at the screen. Carter hit a tab, and up popped the route map.

"It's called the Precipice Trail," Carter told him. He traced the route with his finger. "This part gets really steep, and it ends up on top of a mountain."

"I've never done a hike like that," Nate admitted. "Looks like it could be scary." He grinned. "I'm in."

"Cool."

And just like that, Nate knew there would never be a better time.

"You know when we talked on Sunday?" Nate's breathing quickened. "I… I wasn't entirely honest with you."

Carter frowned. "About what?"

"You asked me if there was someone I was thinking of asking on a date, and I said no." He swallowed. "I lied. You see, what finally brought it home to me this summer that I was bi, was realizing I had feelings for… a guy."

"Oh wow."

"Only, I couldn't tell him, because if it turned out he wasn't into guys, I'd have looked like an idiot, and seeing him every day would only have made it worse."

"Oh. Is it someone I know?" Nate nodded slowly. "Well, are you gonna *tell* me, or is it a secret?" Carter's eyes widened. "Does he *know* you have feelings for him?"

Nate bit his lip. "He does now."

Come on, Carter. You're a smart guy. Work it out.

Carter's frown was still in evidence. "You're not making any sen—" He froze, and Nate's heartbeat went ballistic.

For a moment, neither of them spoke, and Nate was on the verge of slipping into a major panic attack.

Finally, Carter closed the laptop. "Okay. I want you to spell it out for me, because I do *not* want to say something and find out I've gotten this all wrong."

Oh crap.

Nate did his best to calm his quaking heart. "I like you, Carter. I mean, I *really* like you. And I'd like to know you better." Another swallow. "If that's okay with you."

Carter's eyes twinkled. "If that's okay with *me*?" He grinned.

Nate was starting to feel a whole lot better.

"And seeing as it's confession time," Carter continued, "I've got one of my own. You asked if there was anyone on my radar."

"And you said there might be."

Carter nodded. "I lied. There's no *might* about it. There's this guy I share a house with, you see. He's cute, sweet, adorable…."

Nate rolled his eyes. "Oh my God, you've fallen for Dean." Inside he was buzzing. *I don't believe this. I do not* believe *this.*

That earned him a guffaw. "Christ, what a thought." He reached across the bed and took Nate's hand. "Okay. Now what? Do I finally get to ask you on a date?"

Nate's pulse quickened. "Actually? I'd like to ask *you* on one. But… it's a little unusual."

Carter arched his eyebrows. "I can't wait to hear this."

"You know I'm going to my dad's on Saturday for a birthday party? Well, my mom called me a while ago, and said I could bring a guest, and well, you were the first person I thought of, but then I thought there was no way I could ask you to come with me, because a family party? That's just—"

Carter squeezed his hand. "Nate. For God's sake, take a breath."

Nate snapped his mouth shut.

Carter sighed. "I'm still having trouble

believing this is real. I wanted to say something this summer, but you were dating Mia, and that put paid to *that* idea. And then when she dumped you, I wanted to say something *then*, but I was too scared of screwing things up between us. I mean, I couldn't see *you* giving me a smack in the mouth for presuming to even ask you out, but…" His face glowed. "And all that time, you were going through the same thing."

"Kinda funny when you look at it like that, isn't it?" But Carter hadn't answered his question. "If you want to go on a real date, I'd understand."

Carter gaped at him. "As if. A birthday party, where I get to meet your family? I wouldn't miss it. That's what I call a first date to remember. Thank God it's Thursday, and I don't have to wait that long." He hadn't relinquished his hold of Nate's hand. "But I'm not going to wait till Saturday to do this." And before Nate had time to think, Carter leaned over and kissed him, a light brushing of lips, but enough to send Nate's heart soaring.

Then he sat back. "Sorry. I've been thinking about doing that for so long."

Nate's face was on fire. "Don't apologize. Just do it again."

Carter moved as if he had all the time in the world. Their lips met once more, and the second kiss was just as chaste as the first, but that was fine by Nate. Carter inhaled, and it was as if he was breathing Nate in. Then he shifted back with another soft sigh. "I'm not in any hurry to… you know."

Nate smiled, warmth unfurling in his chest. "Slow is good. I've got nothing against slow."

The light in Carter's eyes…. "Perfect."

Then they both jumped as a loud voice called out, "We've got late-night pizza. Come and get it."

Nate laughed. "I could manage a slice."

"Me too."

They got up from the bed and Nate followed Carter to the door. Carter paused. "I didn't just dream the last few minutes, did I?"

Nate kissed him, a darting peck on the lips. "If you did, then so did I."

Part Four

Joel kissed Carrie on the cheek, then shook hands with Eric. "Good to see you again." Laura gave him one of her fly-by hugs before diving to the floor to pet Bramble. Joel rolled his eyes. "She doesn't come here to see me."

"I can hear you, y'know," Laura retorted. Then she went right back to rubbing Bramble's tummy while he lay on his back, all four paws in the air.

"Thanks for the invitation." Eric gazed at the interior. "This is a really cute house."

"We like it."

Finn laughed. "And we'll like it right up to the point where I finish building our dream house."

Eric's eyes widened. "Ooh. Are there plans? Can I see them?"

"Sure." Finn glanced at Joel. "If I can tear them away from Joel. You'll have to excuse the watermarks. He keeps drooling over them."

"I do *not*," Joel declared indignantly.

"Nate won't be long," Carrie told them. "And he's bringing a friend from college. Actually, I think it's one of his roommates."

Joel flashed Finn a look, then pointed to

the back door. "Megan and Lynne are out there, examining the new deck and complaining that this is the first time they've seen it." He met Eric's gaze. "Have you met my sister?"

Eric's eyes twinkled. "No, but I've definitely heard a lot about her."

"It's all true, every word," Finn whispered.

"Why are you whispering?" Joel demanded.

Finn arched his eyebrows. "Because I like my balls where they are, thank you very much."

Joel laughed. He noticed the large white box Carrie had placed on the table. "Oh. Tell me you baked him a cake."

"Of course, and before you ask, it's chocolate, because *duh*, this is Nate."

Finn pointed to the countertop. "Go help yourselves to something to drink. We've got everything. And I do mean everything. I'm sure Joel was expecting at least fifty people to show up today."

"Can I take Bramble out back?" Laura asked.

"Why don't you all go out there, and we'll bring Nate and his guest when they arrive," Joel suggested.

That was all it took to have Laura running toward the back door, Bramble at her heels, and Carrie and Eric following.

When they were outside, Finn arched his

eyebrows. "So how do we play this when he gets here?"

"We act dumb. Carter doesn't need to know Nate has been talking about him. And we don't assume *anything*, you got that?" Joel narrowed his gaze.

"I got it." Finn cocked his head toward the door. "I hear a car. I think the birthday boy is here."

Without a word, Joel headed out onto the front porch. Nate was getting out of the car, and with him was a tall, slim guy with short blond hair.

He brought Carter. Joel hoped this meant what he *thought* it did.

"Hey. Your mom and the rest of the gang just got here." He waited for introductions.

"Dad, this is Carter. He's a friend."

Joel held out his hand. "Then he's welcome here." They shook. "I'm Joel, okay?"

"Good to meet you." Carter appeared relaxed, whereas Nate was a little… bouncy.

"Come on in. I'll introduce you to Finn. Everyone else is out back." Joel cocked his head. "One important question before we get in there."

Carter blinked. "Okay."

"You okay with dog drool?"

Both Nate and Carter burst out laughing. Carter grinned. "I'm good with that. I love dogs. We have three at home."

"Great. You are hereby appointed Dog

Wrangler for the day. Bramble can be a handful."

Nate rolled his eyes. "Dad, we're not kids. Could we take him for a walk maybe? I wanted to show Carter the hotel Finn's been working on."

"Sure." Joel opened the door for them, and they filed inside. "I hope you're both hungry, because there's a mountain of food."

Nate stilled. "Did you make lasagna?"

Finn snorted. "He made enough to last us weeks. Not to mention garlic bread. And *you* had better eat some of that, mister," he added, giving Joel a light tap on his butt. "Because *I'm* aiming to, and I don't want you refusing to kiss me later."

Joel grinned. "As if I would *ever* refuse to kiss you."

Carter cleared his throat. "Where's the bathroom?"

Joel pointed to it, and Carter made a beeline for it. Once he was inside, Joel turned to Nate. "He cut his hair. When did that happen?"

"Couple of days ago." Nate's eyes sparkled. "I like it. I think it makes him look… hot."

Joel raised his eyebrows. "Do I need an update?"

Nate coughed. "Dad."

He held up his hands. "I just want to know what's going on, that's all. If there *is* anything going on."

That sparkle was still there. "There might be?"

Joel laughed. One thing was for certain—Nate looked content.

"Happy birthday!" Laura's squeal shattered the quiet. She ran up to Nate, followed by Carrie and the others.

Carrie shivered. "Too damn cold out there."

"That's what the patio heater is for," Finn commented.

"Well, it would help if someone had turned it on," Megan complained.

"And I would have done, but *someone* didn't ask," he retorted.

Joel glared at them. "Play nice."

Megan opened her eyes wide. "Me? I always play nice."

There was an eruption of chuckles, snickers and guffaws.

Joel watched as Nate was surrounded by his family, on the receiving end of a lot of hugs. When Carter came out of the bathroom, Nate did the introductions, and Carter shook hands with everyone.

Megan's eyes gleamed. "Well he-*llo* there, handsome."

Joel gave her a hard stare. "Down, girl."

"I was just being friendly."

Joel's only response was to snort.

Finn leaned in. "What do you think?" he whispered. "Are they dating?"

Joel observed how Nate's gaze continually drifted in Carter's direction. Carter was doing his fair share of glancing too.

"If they're not now, they will be."

Nate strolled along the sand, unable to stop smiling at the sight of Carter throwing a ball for Bramble. "You'll get tired of that long before he will," he yelled.

Carter's warm laughter carried on the breeze. He picked up the ball and hurled it toward Nate, and Bramble charged after it, his soft ears flapping as he ran. When he reached it, Nate grabbed his collar and attached the leash. He bent down and rubbed Bramble's head. "Good boy. I think Carter's had his cardio for today, don't you?"

Carter walked up to him, smiling, his face flushed. "This is a great beach."

Nate nodded. "This is where Dad walks Bramble every day. I think Bramble could find his way here blindfolded."

Carter's eyes twinkled. "You still feeling guilty because we ditched the party?"

He laughed. "Maybe. Just a little." Carrie, Joel, and Finn were clearing up, Laura had raided the closet for board games, and was currently playing Clue with Eric, Aunt Megan, and Aunt

Lynne.

It had been his dad's idea that they should take Bramble for a walk, claiming he wouldn't have the time. Bramble had been sitting by the front door, staring at his leash and whining.

Nate thought the walk was nothing to do with Bramble, and everything to do with his dad giving them a little space.

He's so cool.

"I like your family," Carter remarked as they headed back to the road. "They seem like nice people."

"They're the best." Nate knew he was lucky: some of his friends at UMA told horror stories about their families.

"Although… your Aunt Megan is a handful."

Nate laughed. "You're a fast learner." He peered at Carter. "How's our first date going?"

Carter came to a halt. "So well, I'm thinking we need a second date. Maybe a movie?"

Nate smiled. "Do I get to hold your hand in the dark?"

"You can hold my hand right now." And with that, Carter took Nate's hand in his, lacing their fingers.

That was *all* kinds of special.

"You okay if we walk like this?" Carter inquired.

Nate was certain he was grinning like an

idiot. "I've got no problems with that."

"So… are you gonna tell your family? About us, I mean."

Nate chuckled. "You think they don't already know?"

"But… how? I mean—"

"Not a lot gets past them. Mom is sharp as a tack. Laura… she guessed about Dad and Finn before they said a word." He laughed. "And don't get me started on Aunt Megan."

"I can see now why you weren't worried about coming out to your parents. They're great."

Yeah, they are.

Carter expelled a soft sigh as they crossed the road. "I don't want this day to end."

Nate's heart beat faster. "It doesn't have to."

Carter frowned. "Huh?"

"Well… Dad has two futons. We could always drive back to Augusta tomorrow. And if we do stay over, Dad might take us to this really great diner in Portland. They do the best breakfast—sausage, scrambled eggs, French toast, home fries…"

Carter groaned. "That's what I call fighting dirty. Would your dad and Finn mind if we stayed?"

Nate shook his head. "They're always telling me I can sleep over." Then he grinned. "Of course, having us sleeping downstairs might put a dent in their plans, but one night won't kill them."

Carter gave him a puzzled glance, then his eyes widened. "Oh, that's…." He chuckled. "You're evil."

"Well, now's the time to decide if you want to date an evil guy."

Carter stopped in the middle of the sidewalk. "Definitely."

Then Nate forgot about the chill wind, Bramble fussing at his feet, and the possibility of being spied on through the blinds of nearby houses, and lost himself in Carter's arms, his warmth, his kiss.

He didn't want the day to end either.

Joel was putting away the plates when Carrie walked into the kitchen. "Can we talk?" she said quietly.

Joel closed the cabinet. "In here? Or someplace private?" She inclined her head toward the living room, where Finn was giving Nate, Carter, Laura and Eric a guided tour of Switch, and Joel chuckled. "They're not going to hear us. What's up?" Megan and Lynne had left, saying they had things to do in Portland.

She inched closer. "Something I need to tell you. I was looking out the window when Nate and Carter came back from walking the dog." She lowered her voice to a whisper. "They were holding hands."

Joel bit back his smile. "How… friendly."

"So Nate's gay all of a sudden?"

Joel shook his head. "Bi, but I'm sure he won't be keeping it a secret for long."

Carrie narrowed her eyes. "You knew all about this, didn't you?"

He gazed back at her with a wide-eyed stare. "Maybe?"

Carrie grinned. "Fine. Then it's *your* turn."

"My turn for what?"

Her smile grew smug. "I gave him the talk all about boys and girls. *You* get to tell him about boys and boys."

She had a point. And seeing as Nate had asked if they could stay, he'd been presented with the opportune moment. "I'll talk to him."

Carrie sighed. "I liked Mia." Before Joel could utter a word, she smiled. "I like Carter too."

"So do I." Most of all, he liked the way Carter looked at Nate. *He already looks smitten.* Not that Nate was any different: he gazed at Carter as if he'd hung the moon.

Carrie took a step back as the others came into the kitchen. Eric glanced at the countertop. "Is there any coffee? I'd love a cup."

"I'll make some," Joel said with a smile.

Laura bounded up to the table with her

usual exuberance. "So, Nate… are you and Carter dating?"

Nate and Carter stared at her, and Carrie's breathing hitched.

Joel gaped. "Sorry, Carter. We forgot to mention Laura has no filters."

"What makes you think they're dating, sweetheart?" Eric inquired.

Laura shrugged. "Well, we came here in the summer plenty of times, and Nate never brought what's-her-name to meet Dad and Finn. So I figured Carter must be important." She met Nate's astonished gaze. "Does this mean you're bi? Because that's cool. Tate McGaskell – he's a boy in my class – he's bi. Right now he's dating Steph Wheeler, but last semester it was Paul Dayton. Everyone thinks he's wicked hot."

Nate and Carter exchanged looks, and then Nate burst out laughing. "I did warn you."

Carrie sighed. "I'm sure that's not how you intended for us to find out, but if it helps, I already had an inkling."

Carter gave Laura a warm smile. "If you must know, this is our first date."

Her mouth fell open, and she glared at Nate. "You couldn't come up with something more… romantic?"

Nate laughed, then glanced at Carter. "You hear that? Our second date needs romance."

"I'll work on it." Carter took Nate's hand

in his, and Joel's heart skipped a beat.

My boy is growing up.

He went back to making coffee, because at least that way, no one got to see his glistening eyes.

It was getting on for five o'clock by the time everyone had left. Joel closed the front door. "At least I don't have to worry about dinner tonight."

Nate laughed. "Let me guess. We're having lasagna."

Finn came out of the bathroom. "There are two new toothbrushes for you. Nate, you know where the sheets, pillows and comforters are."

Carter picked up Finn's console. "Can we play Mario Kart 8 before dinner?"

Finn beamed. "Sure."

Joel laughed. "Great. Now he can beat the pants off *you* instead of me." He grabbed Nate's upper arm. "Come help me in the kitchen." He led him around the corner, and gestured to the fridge. "Help yourself to juice. I'm going to make a salad."

"How is that helping you?" Nate glanced back at the living room as music blared out, and smiled. "Finn's got a friend for life."

Joel pointed to the table. "Sit." He reached into the fridge and pulled out the fixings for the salad, plus the carton of juice. Then he placed a glass in front of Nate. "I'm glad we've got the chance to be alone."

Nate regarded him in silence for a moment, and then narrowed his gaze. "You… you're not gonna give me a talk on sex, are you?" he asked in a low voice.

Damn. "No, I'm not. I'm just going to say two words. Condoms… testing – which needs to become a way of life, by the way – lube, and prep."

Nate folded his arms. "That's more than two words."

"Okay, I lied. We're definitely having the talk. If only because I want to tell you the things I'd wish someone would have told *me*, back when the earth was cooling and I was discovering sex for the first time." He held up his hands. "I know, I know, your mom gave you her version of the talk, but I'd say the focus has changed, wouldn't you?"

Nate bit his lip. "Good point."

Joel forgot about the salad, sat facing his son, and tried to cover everything he felt would be useful to know. He even gave Nate the address of the clinic in Portland where he could get tested. When he was done, he leaned back in his chair. "Any questions?"

Nate gave a sheepish smile. "I think the highpoint of the talk was you saying 'Lube, lube, and more lube.' And I don't have any questions right now, but if I do, I know where to come." He flushed. "They never covered any of *this* in school."

"Don't get Finn started on that. It's a sore point." He smiled. "I like Carter, by the way."

Nate's eyes sparkled. "Yeah, me too."

Then Joel remembered there was something else he'd meant to say. "A word of warning. I know you're not… doing anything now, but it's unrealistic to assume the situation won't change. You're both nineteen, for God's sake."

Nate's flush deepened. "Dad," he protested.

"Having roommates makes a sex life trickier. I speak from experience."

"I'd been thinking about that too. Right now they don't even know we're dating."

Joel nodded. "So either you're both upfront about it… or you're going to be doing a lot of sneaking around. I realize the former option might have… consequences, depending on your roommates, what kind of guys they are. And if you think they're going to have a problem, then… find somewhere else to live. Your mom, Finn and I will be there to support you. Okay?"

Nate swallowed. "Thanks, Dad." He pointed to Joel's knife. "Get me one of those, and I'll help with the salad."

They sat at the table, slicing cucumber and cutting wedges of tomato, and chatted about Nate's classes, his professors, his roommates…

Just to think, ten months ago, everything was so different.

Joel hadn't only found himself a new life with a man he loved – he'd gotten his son back.

Nate lay in the darkness, his arms folded behind his head. Either his dad or Finn was a light snorer: the sound resonated, bouncing off the sloped ceiling.

At least I know they're asleep. Not that he'd thought for one second they'd get up to anything, not while he and Carter were there. He liked the plans for the new house, especially the fact that there would be three bedrooms. And now they'd met Carter, Nate could picture weekends at the new house: an ocean view, a roaring fire, and a room where he and Carter could close the door and shut out the world.

Listen to me. I'm talking as if we're always going to be together.

Nate wasn't stupid. He didn't expect his first boyfriend to be his last. Except there was this little voice in his head that said *Why not?* His dad had found Finn, hadn't he? And there was *nothing wrong* with hoping he and Carter would make it as a couple. Sure, the path might not be an easy one at times, but was *anything* about life easy?

"You awake?" Carter whispered.

Nate chuckled. "I'm lying here having deep thoughts."

"What about?"

He hesitated, then whispered, "You and me."

"Oh, yeah, that *is* deep." There was a pause. "Nate… if I asked you to come over here and get in with me… would you? Just to sleep. I… I wanna hold you."

Oh Lord. It wasn't as if the same thought hadn't crossed Nate's mind. His heartbeat raced.

"It's okay if you don't want to. I mean, I know your dad and Finn are—"

"Hush. I'm coming over." Nate threw the comforter off him, and shivered his way across the gap between the futons. Carter pulled back his comforter, and Nate climbed in. "Ooh, you're warm." Without hesitating, he snuggled up against Carter, his arm across Carter's waist. Carter covered them, then put his arm around Nate.

"Okay. I didn't see *this* coming."

Nate chuckled.

"And I still want to take my time."

"Me too," Nate whispered. He laid his head on Carter's warm, smooth chest. A comforting smell clung to him, the scent of clean sheets and soap.

"Only… when you decide you've had enough of the slow path…"

Nate let out a happy sigh. "You'll be the first to know. Goodnight." Then he reconsidered, and craned his neck, seeking Carter's lips. They kissed, then Carter kissed his forehead.

"Goodnight."

Nate's last thought before sleep took him was to wonder whether he could wake up before his dad, and return to his own bed.

Then he smiled to himself.

He won't be in the least bit surprised.

Part Five

Joel awoke to the smell of fresh coffee, and smiled. He opened his mouth to say thank you, but Finn laid a finger to his lips.

He cuddled up to Joel. "Keep it to a whisper, okay?"

Joel blinked. "Why are we whispering?"

Finn grinned. "Because I want to let them sleep a while longer."

He smiled. "Nate is *not* an early riser."

"I know, but I figured he has a reason to sleep in this morning." Finn's eyes twinkled. "They look so cute, all curled up together."

Joel stared. "Seriously?"

Finn nodded. "I think it's adorable." He speared Joel with a look. "Be honest. If *you'd* gotten the chance to sleep with your first boyfriend, wouldn't you have jumped at it? You and David were younger than Nate and Carter when you first got together."

He sighed. "You're right."

Finn snuggled up closer. "I think they're sweet. I like Carter, even if he *did* beat me at Mario Kart."

Joel sat up and reached for his coffee cup. "So how long do you propose we stay up here?"

"Long enough for them to wake, get up, and have the living room back to normal again, with them acting like they didn't just spend the night in the same bed." Finn took the cup from Joel's fingers. "And in the meantime…" He slid his hand down Joel's torso, making him shiver. When he got to Joel's hard wood, he ran his fingers lightly along its length. "We're gonna play a game."

Joel arched his eyebrows. "And what's this game?"

Finn straddled his hips, reaching behind him to smack Joel's dick against his ass.

"I call it Let's Not Make A Sound."

Nate gave his dad a tight hug. "Thank you. Not just for the party yesterday, but today." Brunch with his dad and Finn had been a lot of fun, and then they'd come back to the house. They hadn't done a whole lot, just lazed around, but he'd lazed around with *Carter*, and that had made all the difference.

"You seem so much happier than you were a week ago. I'm glad." Joel cocked his head. "Have you given any thought to what I said yesterday?"

"Which part?" Nate asked with a grin.

"The bit about telling your roommates what's going on."

Nate sighed. "Carter and I talked about this. We've decided to wait until we've been on another date. *Then* we'll tell them." He knew it made no sense to wait, but neither of them was in a hurry to spill the beans.

"Remember what I said. There are always options."

"We'd better be going." Carter handed Nate his coat, then held out his hand to Joel. "Thank you. It was so good to meet you and Finn."

"As long as you know you're always welcome here," Finn said, walking over to join them. He grinned. "Gotta give me a chance to wipe the floor with you at Mario Kart."

Carter laughed. "You wish." Finn gave them both a brief hug, and Joel opened the front door for them.

"Drive safe. And let me know when you get there."

Nate rolled his eyes. "Dad. I'm nineteen. You can stop worrying about me, you know."

Joel kissed his forehead. "I've got news for you. I'll never stop worrying – I'll just worry less."

Nate and Carter walked to Nate's car. As they opened the doors, Carter smiled.

"You are so lucky, do you know that?"

Nate knew, all right.

"So how did I do?" Carter asked as they opened the door to their suite.

Nate chuckled. "Will you relax? It was a great night. You can't go wrong with pizza, and the movie was awesome. So stop stressing." He glanced toward the living room door, which was closed, then leaned in and kissed Carter on the lips. "I loved our date, okay?" he murmured. Sitting in the dark, holding Carter's hand....

Perfect.

Carter sighed. "It wasn't as romantic as I would have liked. I'll do better tomorrow night."

Nate blinked. "We're going on *another* date?"

Carter nodded. "I'm taking you to dinner. It would've been tonight, but they were fully booked. Tomorrow was all I could get."

"Wanna tell me *where* you're taking me?"

Carter tapped the side of his nose. "It's a surprise. Finn told me about this place." He pulled Nate into his arms. "And I promise, it'll be more romantic than Pizza Hut."

The living room door opened abruptly, and they sprang apart. Dean emerged, carrying an empty pizza box. He came to a halt when he saw them.

"Looking awfully cozy there. Something we should know?" He leered. "Hey, Mike, I just caught Nate and Carter canoodling in the hallway."

Mike appeared a moment later. "You did what?"

Nate glanced at Carter. "That's our cue." He squared his shoulders. "We've just got back from our date."

"Date?" Dean's jaw dropped. "So you're both gay? Whoa."

"I'm gay," Carter said quickly. "Nate's bi."

A slow grin spread over Dean's face. "Hey… if you two wanna make out on the couch… I wouldn't complain."

"You are just a fucking pervert, do you know that?" Mike glared at Dean.

"What?" Dean gave him a puzzled glance. "Two guys together is hot."

Mike shook his head. "Ignore him. It's usually the best way." He smiled at them. "Congrats, guys." He tugged Dean back into the living room. "Leave them alone."

The last thing they heard as the door closed was Dean's plaintive, "But it *is* hot!"

Carter scowled. "Great. Now every time I'm in your room or you're in mine, all I'm gonna be thinking about is if Dean is out there with his ear pressed to the door."

"If it's going to bother you, then we do what my dad suggested, and find someplace else." He grabbed Carter's hand. "My room. Now."

Once they were inside, the door closed, he drew Carter into his arms. "That's better," he murmured, before cupping Carter's head with one hand and tugging him down into a long kiss. When they parted, Nate leaned in, their foreheads touching. "Now that the cat is out of the bag… want to sleep in my bed tonight?"

Carter smiled. "I thought you'd never ask." His lips claimed Nate's, and Nate let out a low moan of pleasure when Carter's tongue sought his.

There was a muffled sound outside, and they both turned to look at the door.

"Goodnight, Dean," they said, as if synchronized.

Nate smothered his laughter as he caught Dean's low "Aw fuck."

When he frowned, Carter kissed him again. "Hey. I know how to make sure Dean gets the message."

"Oh yeah?"

Carter grinned. "Sure. Next time he brings a girl back here, we wait till they're in his room, then stand outside and call out scores, like it's an Olympic event."

Nate gaped. "We can't do that."

Carter's eyes gleamed. "Watch me." He slid his arms around Nate's waist. "Now… where were we?"

Then he obviously remembered, because his lips met Nate's.

The End

Follow Your HEART

A *Maine Men* STORY

K.C. WELLS

Talking To Marcus

Labor Day

Marcus closed the door to the summerhouse behind him and sighed.

I love my family, but God, they can be a handful.

Labor Day weekend was turning out to be a rerun of the Fourth, only with slightly fewer people. His parents were there, of course, plus his sister Jess and nephew Jake, his brother Chris and his kids Sarah and Mike, and his second cousin Ashley and her kids. Seb was a godsend, helping with the cooking, and generally making sure everything went smoothly. Chris had smirked when he learned they were staying in the summerhouse for the weekend.

Marcus was no fool. It was the only place they were guaranteed to get some privacy.

A moment later the door opened, and Seb darted inside. He peered through the blinds in an almost furtive manner.

"What are you doing?" Marcus asked.

Seb whirled around and put his finger to his lips. "Shh. She'll hear you," he whispered.

"*Who'll* hear me?" Marcus whispered back.

"Sophia. She won't leave me alone. First she wanted to play chess, then it was Scrabble…"

Marcus chuckled. "You're hiding from a

nine-year-old *girl*?"

"You better believe I am. And nine years old my ass. I think she was born a teenager."

"Aw. You've got a fan." He nodded toward the door. "If you're serious about escaping detection in here, might I suggest you lock it?"

Seb's eyes widened. "Good thinking." He turned the key in the lock, just as Sophia's clear voice rang out.

"Seb? I know you're in there."

Marcus froze, and Seb backed away from the door slowly. A shadow fell across the blinds, and Seb's breathing hitched. The door handle rattled.

"Sophia?" That was his mom calling. "Come into the house. I'm making a cake."

"Coming." Footsteps sounded on the stone-slabbed path to the house.

Seb whooshed out a breath. "That was a close one."

Marcus had an inkling his mom's decision to bake was for their benefit. *Bless her.*

Seb turned and looped his arms around Marcus's neck. "And now that we're alone…"

Marcus bit his lip. "Just what did you have in mind?" The answer became apparent when Seb snaked his hand down Marcus's front to cup his dick. "You *are* kidding, right?" He shook his head. "I swear, it's like you're permanently in heat."

"I'll be quick. I can get you off in less than five minutes."

He laughed. "Oh, I don't doubt that. I'm just saying your timing is way off." He wrapped his arms around Seb's waist. "Wouldn't you prefer to wait till tonight? When it's just the two of us, with no likelihood of interruptions, and all the time we want to make love?"

"Can't I have both?" There was a plaintive edge to Seb's plea. The door handle rattled again, and he stilled. "Shit, she's back."

"Marcus? You in there?" It was Jake.

Marcus released Seb and walked over to the door. He unlocked it and opened it just wide enough to reach through it and drag Jake into the summerhouse. Then he locked it again. "We're hiding from Sophia—well, Seb is." When that raised only the merest hint of a smile, he frowned. "Are you okay?"

"Not really. I need to ask you a favor."

"Name it." Not that Marcus was all that surprised. Jake had been quiet ever since he'd arrived three days before. Whatever it was that had been troubling him during the summer had obviously not been resolved.

"Do you think I could come visit you, once everyone's gone? Maybe next weekend? I… I need to talk to you."

"Can't it be now? Mom's rescued us from Sophia for a while."

Jake shook his head. "I'd prefer it if it was just the two of us." Then he glanced at Seb. "Okay, the three of us. If two heads are better than one, then why not three?"

"This *is* about that guy? The one you said nothing can happen with?"

Jake's chin quivered and he took shallow, rapid breaths. "Yeah. You said I should tell him how I feel, remember? That once I'd done that, everything would be out in the open, and I could move on."

He nodded. "And you said your worst-case scenario would be him admitting he felt the same way about you." Which still perplexed him. "So what's changed?"

Jake shivered. "I took that job in Boston, that's what. All because I couldn't bear to be so far away from him. But now I can't stop thinking about him. If anything, it's worse than ever."

"How long have you felt this way about the guy?" Seb asked.

There was a pause before Jake replied. "Four years, give or take."

Marcus stared at him. "You left that part out. And he doesn't have a clue how you feel about him?"

Jake paled. "I don't think so. Yeah. I think I'd know if he did."

"Jake? Dad wants you," Sarah shouted from the house.

He sighed. "He's setting up speakers for tonight's movie." The beseeching look in his eyes tore at Marcus's heart. "So… can I come see you?"

As if Marcus could refuse. He wanted to help Jake if he could. And besides, there was a mystery here that he was dying to resolve.

"Sure. I'll be here. Seb too, seeing as he spends his weekends here."

"Great. Thank you, so much." Jake expelled a breath. "Okay. Now I'll go help Uncle Chris." He gazed at the interior of the summerhouse. "You've got yourselves a nice little hideaway here."

"If you need a place to think, or be quiet, or just escape, you're welcome to use it," Marcus told him.

Jake smiled. "Thank you. I'd better go help him." He opened the door and walked out, closing it behind him.

"What the hell is going on?" Seb stared at the door. "He's a mess. This has to be one fucked up situation if it's gotten him *this* screwed up."

"We'll find out at the weekend. In the meantime, we've given him a place to find some privacy—if he needs it." Marcus shook his head. "What I don't get is why he can't just come out and say what's going on. I mean, how bad can it be?"

Sharing a Secret

September 11

As soon as Jake stepped through the front door, he caught a whiff of something burning. "Mom?"

"In the kitchen, making dinner."

Oh God.

"Do I need to go to Walgreens and pick up more Tums? Or maybe have paramedics on standby?" He removed his coat and hung it on a hook by the door.

Mom glared at him as he entered the kitchen. "Hey, I've got an idea. You don't like my cooking? You can always move out and feed yourself." She stood at the stove, stirring something in a pan. "To be honest, I'm surprised you're still here. I was sure you'd want a place of your own now you're working."

"You trying to get rid of me, Mom? Five minutes ago, you were telling me how great it was to have me home from school." He knew she was right. Twenty-two was no age to still be living with his mom.

She turned off the heat under the pan. "Might have to rethink dinner." Her eyes sparkled. "How does pizza sound?"

He laughed. "Sounds good."

Mom reached into the drawer where she kept the takeout menus. "I like having you here, but surely I cramp your style. I mean, if you want to bring someone home, having your mom around is kinda rough. It might put some people off. I know if a boyfriend had asked *me* to spend the night under the same roof as his parents, I would've felt awkward." She frowned. "Didn't Mike mention something last weekend about looking for a roommate?"

"Did he?" That weekend was kind of a blur. He'd spent most of it in turmoil.

"Sure. He had one, but they moved out. You guys could share. You get along great. Maybe you should call him."

He shrugged. "It's an idea." One he didn't want to think about right then.

"Unless you already have a place in mind?"

"You ready to order a pizza?" *Change the subject, Mom.*

She arched her eyebrows. "I will be, once I know what you'd like. And I thought I'd make biscuits and gravy for breakfast tomorrow. Your grandmother's recipe."

Jake bit his lip. "Aw, sorry. I won't be around. I'm getting up early tomorrow. I'm going to see Uncle Marcus." It still felt a little strange to think of him as Marcus.

"But you saw him last weekend."

"He knows I'm coming, okay?"

Mom sighed. "What's wrong, sweetheart?"

Jake stilled. "What do you mean? Nothing's wrong." His pulse quickened. Mom knew him too well.

She wiped her hands, then pulled out a chair and sat. "I've known for a while that something's bugging you. Ever since this summer. I thought spending time with Marcus might help. I know you like him."

"Yeah, I do."

Mom gave him a speculative glance. "I was thinking more along the lines of him mentoring you. Improving your self-confidence. *You* know, so you could share… stuff. Things he'd understand better than I could. And not just because he's a guy, but because he's a *gay* guy."

Aw crap.

"Mom, it's… complicated."

Mom's smile was kind. "What's so complicated about telling me you're not into girls?" She froze. "You're not, are you? Or are my Super Mom Powers really pathetic?"

Jake crouched beside her chair and hugged her. "Your powers still work."

"See?" She held him tight. "Was that so bad?"

If only it were as easy to share what lay in his heart.

"You can tell me anything, honey," she said in a low voice.

He disengaged himself gently from her arms. "No, I can't. At least, not yet."

Mom cupped his cheek. "Will seeing Marcus help?"

"I hope so." It all depended on how he reacted.

"You worry me."

Shit. "That's the last thing I wanna do." He looked her in the eye. "I promise, one way or another, I'm gonna sort this out."

Because he couldn't go on like this.

September 12

Jake stared through the living room windows, watching the squirrel antics. "They're cute, aren't they?"

Marcus chuckled. "This is what I do every morning with my first cup of coffee. I watch them chasing each other around the yard."

"Did someone say coffee?" Seb came into the room, carrying a tray laden with a coffee pot, a jug, and three cups.

"It was good of Grandmomma and Granddad to let you stay here," Jake commented.

"Oops. I forgot the sugar and the cookies." Seb scooted out of the room.

"I'm looking for a place closer to Ogunquit,"

Marcus told him.

"For you and Seb?" When Marcus nodded, Jake smiled. "I'm glad you two have each other."

Seb returned with sugar and cookies. "I kinda like the idea of spending my weekends here." He rolled his eyes. "Who'd have thought Cape Porpoise would grow on me?"

Marcus poured the coffee. "Okay. You're here. Now talk to us. Who is this mystery guy you've had feelings for, for the past four years? And why haven't you told him?"

Here we go.

"The answer to that last question will become obvious once I answer the first." Jake had gotten this far. He sucked in a deep breath. "His name's Mike."

Marcus blinked. "Well, that's going to be confusing at family gatherings, having two Mikes."

Seb stared at Marcus. "Jesus. For a smart man, you can be dumb sometimes."

"What?"

Seb sat beside Jake on the couch. "How serious is this? Are you in love with him?"

"Yeah."

Seb sighed. "You were right. Now I know why you haven't told him."

Marcus spluttered his coffee. "Wait. Mike? Your *cousin*, Mike?"

Seb raised his eyes heavenward. "Hallelujah. You finally got there." He peered at Jake. "Is he into guys? Has he ever said as much?"

"That's all you're going to ask?" Marcus stared at Seb.

"Well, it's the most important question."

"He doesn't talk about personal stuff. To anyone," Jake added.

"That's true," Marcus confirmed. "He's always been a quiet one, while Sarah is more outgoing." He scraped his fingers through his hair. "But can we get back to the part where you're in love with your cousin? Your *first* cousin?"

Jake's heart sank at Marcus's tone. *I knew it.*

"Is it legal in Boston?" Seb demanded. "I don't have a clue about Maine."

"Yes, it's legal," Jake assured him, his stomach clenched.

"But they're *cousins*," Marcus protested.

Seb gaped at him. "So what? It's not as if they're gonna get each other pregnant, right?"

"When it comes to laws about this kind of thing, gay guys don't figure," Jake told him. "In one state, cousins can only marry if they're too old to have kids or if one of them has been sterilized. Which obviously doesn't apply to us."

"Okay, but we're not talking about marriage," Marcus replied.

"No, we're talking about stigma." Jake swallowed.

Marcus regarded him in silence for a moment, until Jake's heart pounded and his stomach roiled. Finally, Marcus sighed. "I can see why you haven't told Mike how you feel."

Jake nodded. "The way I see it, there are only four ways this can go."

"And they are?" Seb sipped his coffee.

"One. He's horrified by me, and I can never face him again. Two. He's *not* horrified, but he tells me he's not into guys, and I have to get on with my life, knowing it'll never be. Three. He's into guys, but not into me. And four. He's into guys, into me, and thinks everyone else can just go fuck themselves." Four options that he'd gone over and over again in his head, countless times.

Option four? That one tore him in two.

Marcus bit into a cookie. "I can understand why you wouldn't want option one," he said after swallowing. "Or two, for that matter."

Jake gazed at him. "Have you calmed down now?"

He nodded. "That part about being too old to have kids brought it home to me. You're right. Those laws don't apply to same-sex couples, do they? And you're right about stigma. I'm sorry I spoke without thinking."

"And *that* is why I love you," Seb said softly. "When you mess up, you admit it." He got up from the couch, walked over to Marcus and kissed him. Then he sat on the arm of the chair. "Okay. Back to you."

Jake drank a little before speaking. "I… I

dismissed option two."

"Why?" Seb asked.

He'd thought about this for such a long time. "I *might* be wrong, but I don't think so."

Seb stared. "He's gay?"

"If he's not, then he could be bi. It's hard to explain it. Just… little stuff. Nothing I could put into words." Except maybe his belief was built on nothing more substantial than hope.

"You're just going by your feelings, aren't you?" Seb said quietly.

Jake nodded. "And option three? That might lead to insurmountable awkwardness." He breathed deeply. "But at least if I tell him, it's out in the open, and I just have to deal with the consequences."

"I think you've already made your mind up to do that," Marcus observed. When Jake frowned, he smiled. "You took the job in Boston, not San Diego."

He was right. "The first step is to talk to Mike, tell him how I feel. Then? Well, then I play it by ear. I've put it off long enough." He locked gazes with Marcus. "Please, don't tell my mom. Or anyone."

Marcus frowned. "I wouldn't do that. But there *is* something I'd like to ask."

"Ask." The worst was over.

"This summer you said the worst-case scenario would be if Mike had feelings for you. Your option four. Want to explain that?"

Jake got up from the couch and walked to the window. He watched the squirrels as they darted through the grass. "If he feels the same, and he wants to be with me… we couldn't keep it a secret." He glanced at Marcus. "Think about your gut reaction. How do you think everyone *else* will react once we tell them?" He took a deep breath. "The way I see it… Mike feels nothing for me, and I deal with the heartache. Or he *does* feel something, and we deal with the fallout. Either way, it'll be a bumpy ride."

"But you're still gonna tell him," Seb surmised.

Jake nodded. "Because not knowing is killing me." He shivered. "And that's why I have to tell him. Not because there's some part of me that hopes he feels the same way. I really don't expect anything to come of it. I just want some relief. This had been eating away at me for so long…"

Seb got off the arm of the chair and gave Jake a hug. "All you can do is follow your heart."

Warmth barreled through him. "Thanks, Seb."

Marcus stood as Seb released him. "Whatever happens, we're here for you."

"Thank you." *Is it too much to hope that the rest of my family is as accepting?*

"When will you go talk to Mike?" Seb inquired.

Now that he'd overcome one hurdle, Jake

felt ready to tackle more. "What's wrong with today?"

Confession

I am such a wuss.

Some point halfway between Cape Porpoise and Boston, Jake had gotten cold feet. His steely resolve to confess everything to Mike had melted into a slightly firm decision to share one thing—his sexuality.

I can't just walk in there and spill my guts. One step at a time.

Sure, he and Mike talked all the time, but not about anything that mattered. Jake steered clear of personal stuff, as did Mike. Maybe Mike possessed some kind of sixth sense that told him to stay off those topics.

But what if he avoids them because that would reveal too much about himself?

Jake dismissed that thought. It was difficult enough dealing with his own worries, without second guessing Mike's motivation too. And he knew it was wishful thinking to hope Mike was hiding similar feelings.

One step at a time.

It was the best way—the safest way. There was no other route to take. Mike was too important to him.

Hell, wasn't this weekend already shaping up to be a real red-letter event? Mom knew he was gay—though by the sound of it, she'd known for a while. Marcus and Seb knew about Jake's predicament. Marcus's initial reaction had been a bump in the road, but he'd come around, thanks to Seb's matter-of-fact view of the world. Where Jake's relatives were concerned, however, Marcus had always been the most enlightened of the bunch. Jake didn't want to contemplate telling anyone else.

Tell them what? There's nothing to tell.

He had to stop getting ahead of himself.

Jake had always been a firm believer in going with his gut, and it had been telling him for a while that not only was Mike into guys, he might also be into Jake. Not that he had any concrete proof. In fact, most of the time it felt as if he was wishing it into existence.

Maybe telling him I'm gay will provoke a reaction.

And if it wasn't the reaction Jake expected—or wanted—then so be it. He'd have to live with that. Silence was no longer an option. He was done hiding.

He pulled into a parking space in front of Mike's apartment on Bryon Road, and turned off the engine. Jake liked this quiet corner of Chestnut Hill. Leatherbee Woods were only a short walk from the apartment, and he and Mike had often gone for a run there. The small lake hidden among its trees was a tranquil spot.

I could use a little tranquility right now.

He got out of the car and locked it, then headed for the main door, his stomach already churning. Mike had an apartment on the second floor, and Jake had only visited it a couple of times. As he reached the top of the stairs, Mike appeared at his front door, smiling.

"Hey. This is a nice surprise. Come on in."

Jake stepped into the small warm hallway. "Did I come at a bad time?"

Mike snorted. "Are you kidding? It's always good to see you." He held out his hand for Jake's coat. "Do me a favor and take your shoes off? My landlord is a tyrant when it comes to his hardwood floors." He was still smiling as he opened the hall closet to stow the coat. "I didn't think I'd see you until the party."

Jake frowned. "What party?"

Mike stilled. "Oh. You don't know about that? It's at the end of this month. Grandmomma's and Granddad's Golden wedding anniversary. I think Aunt Jess and Uncle Marcus are planning it. Dad said something about it."

"Mom hasn't mentioned it." Jake walked into the living room. There was little in the sparsely furnished room: a cream leather couch, a matching armchair, an ottoman, a glass-topped coffee table, one wooden chair against the wall, and above it, the TV. "Wow. This place is looking neater than the last time I saw it."

"That was before Niall left. He made most of

the mess."

Jake couldn't resist. "You kicked him out because he was a slob?"

"He got engaged. Then suddenly he announced he was moving out because he was getting married."

"Fast worker, huh?"

Mike snickered. "Not exactly. I get the feeling it was what Dad would call a shotgun wedding."

"Oops." Jake pointed to the mirrored door that led to the kitchen. "Nice touch." He frowned. "Was that there last time I came over?"

"Yup, but you probably didn't spot it if it was slid open. This apartment has a *lot* of mirrors. They make the place look bigger. Thank God the landlord didn't go as far as putting them on the ceiling in the master bedroom." He slid the kitchen door open. "Want coffee? I was just about to make some."

"That would be great. And maybe a couple of Grandmomma's cookies? That's assuming you haven't already eaten them all since Tuesday." All he'd had that day had been a protein bar during the two-hour drive to Cape Porpoise, and the cookies Seb had given him.

Mike flushed. "There are three left. You can have them." He grabbed a tin from the countertop. "Here." He filled the reservoir with water, then spooned coffee into the filter. "Why did it take you so long to get here?"

"Ah. When I called to ask if you'd be home this afternoon, I didn't tell you I was calling from Cape Porpoise."

Mike turned to face him. "Why'd you go there? Did you leave something?"

"No, I had to talk to Marcus." Jake's heartbeat slipped into a higher gear. *Not sure I'm ready for this.* He peered at Mike. "New glasses?" It was a safer topic.

"Yeah, I picked them up yesterday. What do you think?"

Mike's previous glasses had been like Sarah's, large and round. These were slimmer, more rectangular in shape, with black frames that complemented Mike's dark brown hair and blue eyes. "I like them." That had to be the understatement of the year. They were perfect for Mike's lean face, and with the addition of his five o'clock shadow, they gave him a sexy new look that wasn't helping Jake at all.

"I'm glad your new job is going well," Mike commented as he grabbed two cups from a cabinet.

"How do you know that?"

Mike's lips twitched. "Because you told me? Last weekend?" He rolled his eyes. "Obviously a memorable conversation."

"Sorry. I had a lot on my mind." *Mostly you.*

"You did seem kinda distracted." Mike smiled. "I still think Uncle Marcus is nuts to want to live in Maine. Do you know how freaking cold it gets up there?" He leaned against the countertop. "That's why I was sure you'd take that West Coast job."

"Really?"

Mike nodded. "Better climate. Not that I'm complaining, by the way. I would've missed you."

Warmth surged through him. "Yeah?"

Mike chuckled. "Who else could I talk to about movies, music, books…? Sarah? Fuck that. All she cares about are those reality TV shows, filled with celebrities. I swear, sometimes I'm not sure we're even related." The coffee dripped into the pot, and the aroma was heavenly. Mike reached into the fridge. "Cream?"

"Please." Jake hadn't opened the tin of cookies yet.

"It was great hanging out with you this summer," Mike said in a low voice. "It feels like it was ages ago now."

"We had a lot of fun," Jake agreed. Spending so many days in Mike's company had been awesome. It had also been a torment, especially having to share a sofa bed. *Talk about being shoved into a candy store when you're on a diet.*

"You surprise me." Mike poured coffee into the cups.

"Huh?"

Mike shrugged. "I just had the feeling sometimes that your body was in Maine, but your mind was someplace else."

Jake shook his head. "You always did see

straight through me, even when we were kids." *And please, don't look too closely now, okay?*

Mike's eyes twinkled. "You used to follow me around, remember? Dad called you my little shadow." His face tightened. "That was when he was more laidback, happy even."

"I know this past year has been rough on him. Do you see much of your mom?"

"Now and then. She keeps inviting me to stay with her and her new guy. So far I've said no. Feels too much like I'd be betraying Dad." He sighed. "Maybe your mom is right. Maybe there *is* a Gilbert curse. Maybe we *are* better off being single."

Jake had had enough of being single. He wanted what Marcus and Seb had. The thing was, there was only one man he wanted it with.

"Hey, you okay?" Mike touched his arm. "Here's your coffee." He handed Jake a cup.

Jake's heart hammered. *I've gotten this far.* "There was a reason I took the job in Boston." His throat dried up, and he took a sip of coffee to lubricate it.

Mike grinned. "Let me guess. You'd miss me too."

"Yeah, I would." Another sip. "The thing is… I have… feelings for someone, and they're in Boston."

Jesus, Mike's face… It was as if he couldn't make up his mind if he was happy or sad. "That's… good." His words belied the brief spasm that contorted his features. Then he smiled, but Jake couldn't help noticing it didn't reach his eyes. "Who is she?"

And there they were, at the point of no return.

Jake swallowed. "Not a she. It's a he."

For a moment, Mike said nothing, as immobile as a statue. "Oh," he managed to get out at last. "That was… unexpected." He took a mouthful of coffee. "You kept that quiet. So who else knows?"

"My mom. Although I didn't tell her, she just knew. Must be a mom thing." He gestured to the living room. "Look, can we talk about this sitting down?" *Before my legs give way from under me.*

"Sure." Mike followed him into the next room, and Jake sat on the couch. Mike took the armchair, and the distance between them made his heart ache.

"Marcus knows too, and Seb."

"And now me. I'm flattered." Mike looked him in the eye. "Thanks for trusting me."

"It's not gonna be a problem?" All Jake's instincts were telling him it wasn't, but he had to know.

Mike's face glowed. "*So* not a problem."

His emphatic response ignited a tiny flicker of hope, one that Jake wanted to nurture.

"Now I understand why you went to talk to Marcus," Mike continued. "He'd be the obvious choice." He smiled. "The rainbow sheep of the family. Who came up with that?"

Jake couldn't remember. "He's a good listener." Having him around during the summer had kept Jake sane. Their chats had become a safety valve.

"I like Seb." Mike smiled. "He's a riot." His expression grew wistful. "I envy them." When Jake gave him an inquiring glance, he sighed. "They're so… into each other. The way they look at one another, as if no one else exists." He took another drink. "Is that how you feel about this guy you're interested in?"

It was all Jake could do not to react. "Yeah."

"And does he feel the same way about you?"

Jake's chest tightened. "I don't know." Mike's brow furrowed, and he knew he couldn't leave it there. "It's kinda one-sided."

Mike widened his eyes. "You haven't told him? You're holding a torch for a guy and he's totally oblivious?"

"The whole scenario is… complicated."

"Tell me about it," Mike muttered.

What? "Something you want to share?"

"It's just that… I can't believe you're coming out with all this stuff. Talk about a coincidence." When Jake's only response was to stare at him, Mike sighed. "The thing is… I'm going through a similar situation."

Jake's heart plummeted. "There's someone you're interested in?"

He huffed. "There's been someone for a while. Sarah picked up on it, not that I've told her a damn thing. She knows *something* is going on though." He cocked his head. "But enough about me. You're confident enough to tell me you're gay." He stilled. "Sorry. I shouldn't make assumptions."

Jake smiled. "It's okay. Yes, I'm gay." He wanted to know more about whoever Mike was interested in, but at the same time, he wanted to cover his ears and shout *la la la.*

"Okay. So you've told me, Marcus, your mom knows… If you can admit the truth to *us*, can't you admit how you feel to this guy?"

Just tell him. The urge was overwhelming. "It's not that easy."

Mike's mouth fell open. "Oh God. Is he married?" He placed his empty cup on the coffee table.

"No, nothing like that. He's sort of… unattainable." Christ, he hated this dancing around the houses routine.

"What makes him that?"

Aw crap. "I can't explain, and please, don't ask me to."

Mike held up his hands. "Okay, okay. But… I'm here for you, all right?" His voice was laced with warmth and concern.

"Thanks." It was all Jake could manage.

"No, I really mean it," Mike protested. "We… we're so alike, you and me."

"We get along, don't we?" Jake didn't think they were *that* similar, apart from their shared interests.

"Yeah, but today has shown me it's more than that." Jake stared at him, and Mike locked gazes with him. "You're going through something, and you can't share it. I… I know how that feels."

Jake blinked. "You do?"

Mike nodded. "It's like… having a secret. You want to share it with the one person who would understand, the person who has you all tied up in knots, but you can't. Because to do that would open up the biggest can of worms *ever*."

Jake's throat seized.

Mike leaned forward, hands clasped between his knees, his head bowed. "I swore I'd never tell a soul, but today… something feels different."

Jake's skin tingled, and his pulse quickened.

Mike raised his head. "This guy you've got feelings for… is it serious?"

"Why do you want to know?" The words came out as a croak.

"Because I *have* to know, okay?"

Jake gazed at him. "You're trembling."

"And you haven't answered my question," Mike retorted.

"How can I answer that? Sure, *I'm* as serious about him as it's possible to be, but I can't speak for him."

"I see." Mike's face fell.

Jake's stomach was churning again. "Mike… what is it?" *And why the fuck are you still trembling?*

Mike put his head in his hands. "I'm such a fucking coward."

Jake couldn't stay put a second longer. He lurched off the couch and knelt in front of Mike's chair, his heart aching at the sight of Mike in such distress.

Mike drew in a deep breath. "I told you there's someone I've been interested in for a while."

"Yes." Jake couldn't take his eyes off Mike.

"I haven't said anything because… well… for one thing, I thought I had no chance with them. Until today. Except I might even be wrong about that."

Oh God. He can't mean… "Mike?" *He's not talking about me. He's not.*

Mike lifted his chin, his gaze tortured. "Never been so torn my whole life. With one breath you gave me such hope, and then you robbed me of it with the next."

This isn't happening.

"How did I give you hope?"

Mike didn't break eye contact. "You told me you're gay. Well… me too."

REVELATIONS

He's gay.

He's gay.

I knew it.

It took every ounce of effort Jake possessed not to fist-pump the air.

"Since when?" *And why haven't you said anything before now?* Except Jake was just as bad. He got up off the floor and retook his seat on the couch. "Does your dad know?"

Mike sagged against the armchair's cushions. "No one knows, except you. And I wouldn't have told *you* if you hadn't come out with it first." He gave a half smile. "See what I did there? And as for how long I've been gay?" He shrugged. "Up until recently, I'd have said I was just experimenting."

"So you… *have been* with guys." Jake's stomach churned at the thought of Mike in someone else's arms, in someone's bed… Mike telling some guy he loved him…

"Yeah. I guess I got curious in college. There were a few guys. Some of them were gay, others were just… playing with sex. So I played too."

"Did you ever date girls?" Jake couldn't recall Mike dating anyone, but he figured there had to have been someone in college.

Mike shook his head. "You'd think that was a big clue right there, huh? Whenever Dad asked if there was anyone, I lied, told him I'd gone out a couple of times with a girl. It seemed easier that way. If he'd gotten curious, he might've started asking questions, and I didn't have any answers. So there I was, away from Dad, from Sarah, surrounded by some *really* gorgeous guys…"

Jake had a few questions of his own. *Who was your first? How did you meet these guys? This person you're interested in… is it serious?* Except he didn't want to hear the answers.

"My roommate was gay. I think I was just… convenient, you know? He was horny, *I* was horny… That was how it started. Like I said, I was curious. And then, once I graduated, I hooked up with guys I met on Grindr."

"You're on Grindr?" Jake's heart sank, his elation at Mike's coming out dissipating.

"Sure." Mike frowned. "What's wrong with that? I mean, I know *you're* not. I would've seen you on there if you were." He bit his lip. "Even if you'd used another name, I'd know your body anywhere." Jake blinked, and Mike flushed. "You know what? This came out all wrong. There weren't *that* many guys. I mean, we're talking less than five, all right? But there was always part of me that said I wasn't gay."

"What changed your mind?"

Mike fell silent for a moment before pushing

out a sigh. "I've gotten this far, I might as well come out with the rest of it." He leaned forward, elbows balanced on his knees. "It was just sex, okay? And I was happy with that. Until…"

"Until?" Jake's stomach was still in knots.

"I realized something. I wanted more. I didn't care for *any* of those guys, not the way I cared for…."

Jake's heartbeat quickened, and blood pounded in his ears.

"Anyway, I started looking for someone who made me *feel.* And you know what? No one came along. No one could hold a candle to…"

Jake's heart couldn't stand much more. "For Christ's sake, Mike, will you just finish a fucking sentence?"

Mike stared at him. "*You*, all right? I didn't care for any of them, the way I care for you. Not *one* of them made me feel the way you do. No one even came close. And it was then I realized I *must* be gay, because I was in love with a guy."

In love… Oh fuck.

Mike swallowed. "I knew I didn't want anyone else. Only you. So when you said you were gay…" He drew in a deep breath. "I'm happy for you, really I am. I'm glad you've found someone to love. Now all you need to do is tell him how you feel." He locked gazes with Jake. "Trust me. He's getting a great guy. And I know you said he's unattainable, but *Jesus*, there has to be a way, so find it. Life is too fucking short to not seize every chance we get to be happy."

Jake's heart hammered. "Okay. I'll tell him." His legs shook as he got up off the couch and knelt in front of Mike.

"What… what are you doing?" Mike's eyes were wide.

Jake raised his chin and looked him squarely in the eye. "Telling you… I love you. That I've loved you ever since I was eighteen, when I realized no one would ever make my heart beat as fast as you did." He gave a hard swallow. "I didn't want to tell you because I know nothing can come of it. You know that too. You said as much. We'd be opening up the biggest can of worms *ever*."

Mike gazed at him, his expression fixed in a mixture of joy and dismay.

Jake got to his feet. "I came here today because I had to tell you how I feel. Holding it inside me for so long was eating me alive. Okay, I'm done. I might have *hoped* you felt something for me, but I never expected it. And now we get to live with it."

"*Live* with it?" Mike lunged out of the armchair. "Wait a minute. You're… you're gonna leave it there? You know I'm in love with you. You just told me you love *me*. That's not an ending, that's a beginning."

Jake gaped at him. "That can of worms you mentioned? It has a label, and we both know what it says. Cousins."

"And what if… what if we don't open it?"

Christ, his heart… "What does that mean?"

Mike's chest heaved. "We don't tell anyone. We keep it a secret. No one needs to know."

"Someone *already* knows, remember? Marcus? Seb?"

"You think they'll tell anyone?"

Jake breathed deeply. "No, they won't. They said so."

"Then why not?" Mike gripped his shoulders, his eyes fixed on Jake's face. "Do you *want* to walk away? Really?"

Oh God.

Jake was trembling. "No," he whispered.

"You said you've loved me since you were eighteen. Well, I've loved you like a brother all my life. It's taken me the last few years to realize all the *other* ways I wanted to love you. I've dreamed about you."

His legs were about to give way. "I've dreamed about you too," Jake croaked.

"And we're not doing anything wrong, okay? I love you. How can love be wrong?"

Jake swallowed again. "I can think of a few people who might argue with that. Namely, everyone in our family, except Marcus, and *he* struggled at first."

"Then we don't tell them." Mike looked him in the eye. "This is just between us. Our secret. Please, Jake, I can't walk away. Not now I know how you feel. If you knew how much I want you… So much, it hurts."

"I want you too, but…" His heart quaking, Jake bared his soul. "There hasn't been anyone. I haven't—"

Mike let out a long breath. "Oh God."

For one glorious moment, Jake allowed himself to hope. *A secret. It has to stay a secret. But we could…*

"So, all those other ways you just mentioned…." Jake cupped Mike's face, his heart hammering. "You think you could show me a few of them?"

Mike smiled. "Oh yeah. As soon as I've done this." His hands were gentle on Jake's nape as he drew him closer, and warm lips met Jake's in a sweet kiss. "God, how I've waited to do that," he murmured against Jake's lips.

"Then keep going," Jake whispered. "This is my first kiss, and I don't want it to end."

Mike's breathing hitched. "You were serious. You're really a virgin?"

Jake straightened. "What's wrong with that?"

"Oh God, absolutely nothing." Mike's face glowed. "I like the fact that I get to be your first." He bit his lip. "That came out all wrong again. I shouldn't make assump—"

Jake covered Mike's mouth with his hand. "Make all the assumptions you like. I haven't waited this long to be with anyone but you. And I don't intend waiting anymore." He removed his hand and pressed his lips to Mike's. "I'm yours, Mike. All of me." The words came out in a whisper.

Mike hauled Jake to his feet, grabbed his hand, and pulled him toward the door Jake knew led to his bedroom. Jake's heart pounded, and he was aware of a sudden rush of warmth spreading outward from his groin.

He wants me.

Once inside, Mike drew him close and kissed him again, tentative kisses that slowly built until Jake's hand was on Mike's neck, pulling him closer, needing more.

"I can't tell you how long I've wanted to do this," Mike whispered, making Jake shiver as he kissed his neck, his lips soft and warm.

"I can't believe this is happening," Jake murmured, his hands on Mike's back, holding him against his body, feeling Mike's heat.

"Finally." Mike kissed him hungrily, one hand on Jake's hip, rubbing him, tugging Jake's shirt free of his jeans. He nuzzled Jake's neck, sliding his hands under the fabric to stroke bare skin. His rough chuckle tickled.

"What's so funny?"

Mike straightened, and Jake couldn't see his eyes. "My glasses. You steamed 'em up."

Jake laughed. "Take 'em off. They're for distance anyway, and I'm planning on getting up close and personal." His lighthearted words belied the thumping of his heart, his rapid pulse, the tremors that trickled through him at the thought of feeling Mike's naked body against his.

Mike removed them and placed them on the nightstand. He held Jake's face between his hands and looked at him so gravely that Jake's palpitations increased. "We need to talk. Before we take another step."

"Okay." Christ, his heart felt as if it was going to burst.

"The guys I've been with," Mike began, and Jake's stomach clenched.

"We're gonna talk about them *now*? It's okay. I'm glad you have more experience than I do. There. We're done."

"No, we're not." Mike's voice was gentle but firm. "Some of them were on PrEP—you know what that is?" Jake nodded. "The others used condoms. Now, I haven't been with anyone in a while, but I want us to use condoms, at least until I get—until *we* get—a clean bill of health." Jesus, his eyes… Jake couldn't look away. "But you need to know… once we get the all clear, we're gonna ditch the gloves. You're the only one I want, you got that?"

"I got it." The words came out in a strangled whisper. "This… this is for real, you and me."

"You got that right." Then Mike claimed his mouth in a fervent kiss, Jake's arms locked around his neck. Mike pushed him against the mirrored closet door, and Jake had to grip the door frame as

Mike unbuttoned his shirt, pulling aside the flaps to reveal his torso. He trembled when Mike bent to flick Jake's nipple with his tongue before laying a path of kisses over his abs to the waistband of his jeans. Mike knelt in front of him, grinning. "The showoff in me wants to unfasten these with my teeth, but the realist part keeps telling him not to be so fucking stupid."

Jake's breathing quickened as Mike popped the button free, lowered the zipper, then eased his jeans past his hips to reveal Jake's tightening briefs, his erection pushing at the cotton, jutting out toward Mike's lips.

Then his jeans and briefs were at Jake's ankles, Mike's hand was curled around Jake's dick, and Mike's warm mouth enveloped the head. Jake held onto the door frame, alternating between closing his eyes to enjoy the sensation, and staring at Mike, mesmerized by the sight of his own rapidly stiffening cock sliding between Mike's lips. Jake stepped out of the puddle of fabric, widened his stance, and stroked Mike's head and shoulder, his tremors multiplying.

"God, it's so thick," Mike gasped as he pulled free. "You're gonna feel so good inside me."

Jake grabbed Mike's shoulders. "Wait." His heartbeat raced. When Mike looked up at him, Jake swallowed. "What if… what if I want you inside of *me*?"

Mike's slow smile sent a quiver through Jake's belly. "Then Christmas really has come early."

He went back to sucking Jake's cock, only now, he was trying to undress himself without breaking the connection, almost falling over in the process.

Jake chuckled. "You *can* come up for air, you know." Any more words died in his throat when he caught a glimpse of Mike's dick, long, heavy, and flushed. Then Mike too was naked, his hand working his own shaft as he sucked on Jake's balls. "Fuck, you're sexy."

Mike's gaze met his. "Right back atcha." He took Jake into his mouth, moaning around his girth as his hand slid up and down his own dick. Mike gasped. "God, I'm like a rock." He gripped his cock. "Want to feel your mouth on me."

Jake's breathing hitched. "I want that too."

Mike sprang to his feet, tugged Jake across to the bed, and shoved him onto it. "On all fours."

Jake did as instructed, his heart thumping as he got that first taste of Mike's dick.

"Teeth, baby. Be careful of the teeth, okay?"

Jake cursed himself for his lack of experience. He tried again, and Mike's groans of pleasure made him soar. Then he caught sight of himself in the closet door mirror, and heat flushed through him. Naked, his shaft pointing like a goddamn arrow, bobbing stiffly with each suck on Mike's dick…

Mike followed his glance. "Look at you. At us."

Jake took a breath. "If I do that, this'll be

over real quick." He went back to worshipping Mike's cock, doing his best to replicate Mike's actions, his heart almost bursting with pride when Mike grabbed hold of his head and held him steady, Mike's hips bucking as he fucked Jake's mouth, never once venturing too deep.

Jake paused between sucks, panting. "I think I just found a new hobby."

Mike bent and kissed him, his tongue parting Jake's lips. "As long as I'm the only one you wanna practice on."

Jake smiled. "You'd better believe it." He flicked the taut head of Mike's cock with his tongue, loving the noises that poured from Mike's mouth. Jake tugged on his own dick, his fingers sticky with precum as he licked along Mike's stony shaft. "Think I could get off just from sucking you," he confessed.

"Can't have you coming yet," Mike gasped. "Not until I'm inside you." He yanked open the nightstand drawer and rummaged in there for a moment before letting out a triumphant yell. "There's two left." He held a couple of condom packets close to his face.

"What are you doing?" Jake demanded.

"Making sure they haven't expired."

"And?"

Mike beamed. "Next year. We're good to go."

"You've only got two?"

Mike rolled his eyes. "Then we'll go

shopping for more." He removed a bottle of lube too and dropped it onto the comforter. "Lie on your side across the foot of the bed, and grab the foot rail."

Jake complied, drawing his right knee up toward his chest, his foot braced against the metal bed frame. Mike lay behind him, his arms around Jake as he kissed his neck, his shoulders, his upper arms.

"First we do this," Mike whispered, and Jake shuddered as a slick finger pressed against his pucker. "Nice and slow. Gotta open you up a little."

Jake held onto the footboard with both hands as Mike slid a finger into him, taking his time. "Is this the moment where I tell you I *have* played with my ass?"

Mike chuckled against Jake's neck. "Good to know." He fingered Jake, until Jake was in constant motion, fucking himself on it. Mike added another finger, and *Christ*, Jake felt full. Mike stilled inside him, and Jake was thankful for the breather.

"Feels thicker than my dildo. Which is a very *skinny* dildo, I have to tell ya."

Mike's breath warmed his shoulder. "I have a really thick one you might wanna try."

"Please, tell me you're talking about your cock." Then Jake groaned as Mike moved his fingers in and out, and he gripped the rail even tighter. "Feels good."

"This will feel better." Mike withdrew his fingers, and the *tear* of a wrapper behind him had

Jake's heartbeat quicken. Mike snuggled up to Jake's body. "Ready?"

"*So* ready." He strove to relax as Mike entered him, his breath catching as the head popped through the ring of muscle, stretching him. Mike's hand was on his hip, and Jake let go of the railing to lace their fingers as Mike slowly filled him to the hilt. "Oh God."

"Wanted this for so long," Mike whispered, kissing his neck. He held still, and Jake clutched Mike's hand. The stretch took his breath away, and he inhaled deeply, willing his body to relax a little more. When Mike finally began to move, Jake was ready for him.

"Feels so good," he admitted. Mike kept his thrusts slow and measured, and when he nudged Jake's gland, it felt as if the world exploded into Technicolor. Jake turned his head to meet Mike's kiss, and there they were, joined at last.

"Look." Mike inclined his head toward the closet door.

Jake craned his neck, and—*Sweet Jesus, look at us.* He watched as Mike's cock slid in and out of his hole, glistening with lube. He couldn't look away, his gaze locked on Mike's thick shaft spearing into his body. Jake reached down, his fingertips grazing the latex-covered cock as it slid into him. Then Mike stilled, and Jake did the work, rocking back and forth on that meaty dick.

They took it in turns, both of them staring at

their reflections, the sight adding fuel to the fire that already consumed Jake. When Mike pulled free, Jake groaned, until Mike pushed him onto his back, and pulled on his legs, changing his position. Jake raised his arms and grabbed the bed rail above his head, while Mike shoved a pillow under Jake's hip, rolling his ass up off the comforter. He guided his cock back to Jake's hole and filled him in one long thrust. Then he hooked his arms under Jake's knees and began to rock.

Jake reached for his dick. "Not gonna last much longer," he moaned.

Mike kissed him. "Me neither. You are so fucking *tight*." He grabbed the bottle of lube and squeezed a few drops onto Jake's shaft. Then Mike picked up the pace as Jake worked his dick, tugging on it, his body tingling.

"No," he groaned as warmth spattered his stomach.

Mike's lips were on his in a heartbeat. "It's okay, baby. We're gonna do this again… and again… and again…" He stiffened, and Jake exulted to feel the throb of Mike's cock inside him. Mike buried his face in Jake's neck, and Jake clung to him, his legs wrapped around Mike's waist, caging him, not letting him go.

Never gonna let you go.

Dealing With Reality

September 18

Jake walked out of Mike's bathroom, a towel wrapped around his hips, his hair damp. Mike sat on the bed, smiling. "Do you know how sexy you look when you've just had a shower?"

"What's sexy about being wet?"

Mike bit his lip, pointing to Jake's crotch. "A hard-on, pushing against a towel, that's what." He grinned. "You want me."

Jake rolled his eyes. "Duh. I always want you." It felt as if they'd done nothing but fuck for the past week. Jake left work and drove straight to Mike's apartment, and within five minutes of walking through the front door, they were naked and in Mike's bed.

We're just playing catch-up, that's all. And while he loved the frantic pace, the squeak of Mike's bed, the occasional *thump thump thump* when it banged into the wall, what stilled his heart were those moments when time slowed to a crawl, and they lay together, arms entwined, both whispering words of love.

Jake had waited four years to say those words, and he didn't think he'd ever tire of repeating them. Hearing them fall from Mike's lips?

Heaven.

That evening, however, Jake had resisted the urge to tear Mike's clothes off, and had headed for the shower instead. Thinking was easier under the stream of hot water.

We can't keep doing this.

"Why can't we?" Mike was so still.

Jake blinked, then realized he'd spoken the words aloud. He sighed. "We need to talk." He gestured to Mike's clothed state. "And the fact that you're still dressed tells me you know I'm right."

Mike said nothing for a moment, and Jake knew he'd nailed it. "You go first," Mike prompted.

Jake sat on the edge of the bed. "This last week has been crazy, hasn't it?"

That got him a nod. "Crazy—and amazing."

"But it's brought a couple of things home to me," Jake continued. "I've loved coming over here every night, but there comes the time when I have to go home."

"I hate that part," Mike murmured.

"Me too. And then when I get home, Mom gives me the third degree. Why am I working so late every night? I'll burn out if I keep going like this. I need to take some me time."

"Whereas we both know what you *really* need is to take *me*, twice a night," Mike announced. "After meals. Before meals. Or I take you. I'm easy."

Despite the unease in his belly, Jake smiled. "You're insatiable, you mean?"

Mike's eyes gleamed. "Pot… meet kettle."

"My point is… I'm living two lives, and I hate it. When I'm at work, I think about you. When I'm home, I think about you. Two or three hours here during the week, more on the weekend… and always having to lie about it to Mom."

"Hey, we agreed, didn't we? It has to be a secret."

Jake nodded, his chest tight. "Yes, we agreed. And I still think it was the right decision. It's just that the decision is killing me."

Mike sat back against the pillows, his arms wide. "Come here."

Jake got onto the bed and snuggled up to him, his arm around Mike's waist, his head against Mike's chest. He breathed Mike in, comforted by his warmth and the arms that held him. "This is my happy place, okay?" Jake whispered into Mike's chest.

"Mine too. And I think I have the solution that will solve both your issues."

Jake craned his neck to look at Mike's face. "I'm all ears."

Mike smiled. "It's obvious. Move in with me."

"Move in—" Jake blinked. "Wouldn't that make it kinda obvious?"

"Why would it? Everyone in the family knows I'm looking for a new roommate. I said so at the party." He coughed. "Actually, I said it hoping you'd jump at the idea, but you didn't bite."

"Can I be honest? I didn't even hear that. I was so wrapped up in angst, guilt, nerves…" And now that he thought about it, Mom had mentioned it too.

Mike kissed the top of his head. "You hadn't done anything to feel guilty about."

"Ya think? I felt guilty just *thinking* about what I wanted to do to you."

"Have we tried everything you wanted to do?"

Jake smiled. "Nope. Not even close."

Mike's chuckle reverberated through his chest. "Okay, forewarned is forearmed. But *my* point is… it would be the most natural thing in the world if we shared an apartment. No one would be the least bit surprised. And apart from us, only two people would know what was really going on behind closed doors." He smirked. "Well, they wouldn't know for sure, but they'd have a strong suspicion." He cupped Jake's chin, lifting it. "No more having to come up with explanations for your mom. No more having to leave me every night. You'd have your own room, but you'd never have to spend a single night on your own, if you didn't want to. This bed is plenty big enough for two." He kissed Jake softly on the lips. "Well? What do you think?"

Jake's heart soared. "I love it. I can't think why I didn't think of it sooner."

"*I* know why." When Jake gave him an inquiring glance, Mike grinned. "You've been a little… busy."

Ain't that the truth?

"So when do you think you could move in?" Mike asked.

Jake grinned. "What's wrong with tomorrow? It's Saturday, after all. You could come over and help me pack up all my stuff. We could do it in a couple of trips if we use both cars."

Mike snorted. "You don't think that's maybe a little fast? What will your mom say when you go home tonight and announce you've moving out the following day?"

He chuckled. "If I know Mom, it'll be something like, 'I'll help you pack.' She's been making all these Why-haven't-you-found-a-place-of-your-own-yet noises. She can't complain if I follow her suggestions, can she?" He gazed at Mike. "Unless that's too soon for you?"

"Are you kidding? I'm gonna kick you out the door ASAP, because the sooner you're home, the sooner you can tell her the good news."

Jake slid his hand down Mike's front to his sweats, where something obviously hard and thick lurked beneath the soft layer of fabric. "Do you want me to go right away?"

Mike's breathing caught. "Not just yet. Maybe after I've had the chance to indulge in *my* new hobby."

"And what's that?"

His eyes glittered. "Eating your ass until you

come."

Jake unfastened the towel, tossed it aside, and knelt on the pillows, knees wide apart. Mike slid further down the bed, until his head was right where Jake wanted it. When Mike pulled his cheeks apart and he felt that first broad swipe of Mike's tongue over his hole, Jake shivered and grabbed the bed rail. "Gotta love a man who has hobbies."

September 19

Jake stretched, his back aching a little. "Is there any space left in the car?" he asked as Mike came back into the bedroom. They'd already made one trip, both cars laden with boxes and bags.

"No, thank God." When Jake stared at him with raised eyebrows, Mike rolled his eyes. "Don't forget, we still have to find room to put all this. My apartment walls are *not* made of elastic."

Jake grinned. "We can store most of it in my room. After all…." He didn't need to finish the sentence.

Mike gaped. "Oh, *I see*. I'm not just gaining a roommate, I'm losing my personal space." His grin belied his words, however. "Don't worry. There's a third bedroom that only has my desk in it. It's the smallest one. We can use that."

Jake walked over to him, listening out for

signs of Mom coming their way. "It's *your* bedroom, okay? You only have to say the word, and I—"

Mike stopped his words with a kiss. "Yes, it's my bedroom—and I want you in there with me. Yes, there'll be nights when one or both of us might need a little space, and that's why we each have our own rooms. I'm not stupid enough to believe this is gonna be plain sailing, all right? Two people, sharing an apartment, living in each other's pockets… There are bound to be teething troubles. But we'll get through them."

Jack looped his arms around Mike's neck. "You really believe that, don't you?" Mike's conviction rang out so clearly.

Mike nodded, then cupped Jake's nape, pulling him into a lingering kiss. "Christ, you've done it again," he muttered against Jake's lips. "You've steamed my glasses up."

Jake chuckled. "Not my fault. Blame it on those thoughts racing through your brain. Go on, deny it. You're thinking about me naked, aren't you?"

Mike laughed softly. "I'm *always* thinking about you naked." Then he sprang back as Jake heard footsteps in the hallway.

Mom came into the bedroom and beamed. "Wow. Now I need to think what I'll do with all this space."

"Craft room?" Mike suggested.

Both Jake and his mom snorted. "You really

don't know her, do you?" Jake said with a grin. "That's about as likely as her turning it into a home gym."

Mom narrowed her gaze. "Well, I *was* about to order pizza for dinner, but now…"

"I was joking, honest." Jake could backpedal with the best of them.

"And I was being serious," Mike added. "Nothing wrong with a craft room, is there?"

Mom laughed. "Relax. Pizza is still on the menu. You two going to join me, or are you going to eat at Mike's place?"

"At *our* place," Mike corrected. He glanced at Jake. "What do you think?"

Jake wanted to get out of there, in a hurry to start his new life, but he could afford to wait a while. One look at Mom's face told him that while she might have whooped and hollered when he'd shared his news, the sight of his now empty room had brought it home.

Her chick was finally leaving the nest.

"Pizza sounds good."

Mom beamed once more. "Great."

"You ordering from The Real Deal?" he inquired. When she nodded, Jake counted off on his fingers. "Then we can have either the BBQ pulled pork, or the Meat Lovers, and don't forget the chicken fingers with honey ginger sauce, buffalo wings with hot sauce, spicy curly fries, mozzarella sticks—"

Mom held up her hands. "You know what? I'm gonna let you two do the ordering. But it'll be my treat."

"I'll put the order in," Mike announced, heading for the door.

"Menu's in the kitchen, on the fridge," Mom called after him. As soon as Mike was out of sight, her expression softened. "Still can't believe you're moving out."

Jake laughed. "Well, you dropped enough hints."

"Sure, but I didn't think you were listening!" They both chuckled at that. Mom sighed. "This is the right thing to do. Ever since you came home last night and told me Mike had asked if you'd share the apartment, you've seemed… happier." She glanced toward the door. "Makes so much sense. You two have been joined at the hip since you were three and Mike was six. And once you've settled, I'll come visit."

Jake's pulse quickened. "Be sure to call first? Just in case we're out."

Mom snickered. "What you *really* mean is, so you have time to clean."

Sure, let's go with that.

Jake placed his hand on his heart. "Aw crap. You saw right through me."

"Food'll be here in thirty minutes," Mike yelled from downstairs.

Mom pulled Jake into a tight hug. "I have a

confession," she whispered.

"Uh-oh."

She released him, chuckling. "Nothing bad, I promise. It's just… This summer, I asked your uncle Marcus to talk to you. I was worried about you."

"I know you were, and I'm sorry I put you through it. I'm okay now, really."

She brushed his hair back from his forehead. "I know you are. I can see it, plain as day. I gather telling Marcus helped you sort out whatever it was that was bothering you."

"Yeah, it did." Jake smiled. "Everything is gonna be just fine."

As long as one particular secret remained buried.

Mike closed the door, and Jake heaved a sigh of relief. "We did it." He walked slowly toward Mike, locked his arms around Mike's neck, and kissed him, not bothering to rein in the desire that had been building all day. He'd been tempted to take a break during one of their unloading sessions, but Mike had suggested waiting until they were done.

Mike returned his kiss, moving his hands lower to grasp Jake's ass and mold their bodies together, rolling his hips sinuously, allowing Jake to feel the hardness that pushed against his own solid erection. "Love you," Mike said quietly.

"Love you too." So much that Jake's heart ached. It still felt like a dream. The man he'd loved for so long, was holding him, kissing him…

Loving him.

"Bed?" Mike murmured. "Because all of this can wait until tomorrow."

"Bed," Jake agreed. As Mike took him by the hand and led him toward the bedroom, Jake chuckled. "Elizabeth Barrett Browning had to have been a really kinky girl, you know."

Mike came to a halt and turned to stare at him. "Since when do you read Elizabeth Barrett Browning?"

Jake rolled his eyes. "We read her in high school, and again in college. Anyway, there's this poem that begins 'How do I love thee? Let me count the ways.'" He grinned. "I've been counting *our* ways, and we're not done yet."

Mike laughed. "I'm pretty sure that wasn't what she meant."

Jake curved his hand around Mike's cheek. "But if I can be serious for a minute?"

Mike stilled. "Of course."

"I don't know why that poem came to mind today. I looked it up, because something was nagging me. And then I saw the last line, and it hit me." He smiled. "She could've been writing about me—and the way I feel about you."

"Tell me." Mike locked gazes with him.

Jake pulled the line from his memory. "'I love thee with the breath, smiles, tears, of all my life; and, if God choose, I shall but love thee better after death.'"

Mike's breathing hitched. He grasped Jake's hand and led him into the bedroom. "Then come here and let me show you how much I love you."

Out Of The Mouths Of Babes…

September 26

Jake took a last look at the living room. "You don't think it's too subtle, do you? I mean, do you think Grandmomma and Granddad will be able to see it?" There were banners, gold balloons and gold ribbons *everywhere*. It had taken him and Mike an hour to decorate the room.

Mom squinted at him. "You're not too big to get your ass spanked, remember that." Then she smiled. "You boys did a great job. Now clean up your mess, because it won't be long before everyone starts piling through the front door."

Jake glanced at the clock above the fireplace. It was eleven-thirty. "What time are the guests of honor arriving?"

"Marcus said he'd told them to get here by five."

"And they still think they're just coming for some special dinner Marcus and Seb are cooking?" If Jake had been in their shoes, he'd want to know why the family wasn't throwing a party to celebrate their fifty years of marriage.

Mom rolled her eyes. "Have you any idea

how much organizing this has taken? The whole family had to be in on the secret. I'm amazed none of them let something slip. They all had to come up with some activity or other that would take up their time. As far as Mom and Dad know, everyone in the Gilbert family is busy this weekend."

Mike walked into the living room, carrying two bottles of iced tea. He handed one to Jake. "I bet that hurt."

Mom winced. "Yeah. Marcus said they were a little upset. But the way I see it, they'll get over the hurt and disappointment when they walk into this room and everyone yells, Surprise!"

Mike glanced at his surroundings. "*How* many are coming?"

Mom counted off on her fingers. "My cousin Robert is bringing Aunt Carol."

Jake grinned. "I bet the folks at the nursing home are grateful for that. A day without her." That earned him a hard stare from Mom. "Oh, come *on*. You know I'm right. They're all terrified of her. Will she be staying here?"

Mom shook her head. "Robert has got her a hotel room, and he says he'll stay with her. Oh, and your second cousin Josh will be here too."

Jake had pleasant memories of spending time with Robert when he was little. Great Aunt Carol was a prickly old lady of eighty, who seemed to have no filters, or at least, that was how Jake remembered her. It had been a while. "Who else?"

"My cousin Lisa is coming, and this time both Ashley and Matt will be here. Matt called to say he's bringing his girlfriend, Donna. And of course Alex and Sophia will be here."

Mike chuckled. "Someone hide Twister, please? There won't be room for us to play, and Sophia kept bringing it out this summer."

Jake laughed. "Grandmomma hid it, and Sophia found it every time." He did the math. "So, with Dad, Sarah, Marcus and Seb, that makes sixteen adults and two kids."

Mom grinned. "As far as Aunt Carol is concerned, anyone in their twenties is still a kid."

"And does everyone know to park their cars out of sight?" Mike inquired.

Mom nodded. "That's why they're coming early." She sank onto the couch. "I'm exhausted."

Jake guffawed. "How can you be tired? All the food is catered, and they'll be delivering it in a couple of hours. Marcus and Seb cleaned the house from top to bottom. Me and Mike decorated. Mike set up the fireworks in the yard." He put his hands on his hips. "What exactly did *you* do?"

She glared at him. "I had to make sure every sheet, blanket, pillowcase and towel was washed, that's what. And I still haven't worked out where I'm going to put everyone."

"Just make sure the kids are in the attic room, okay?" Sophia was a regular little Tasmanian devil. "Marcus and Seb will be in the summer house, I suppose."

Mom nodded. "So maybe it's a good thing Aunt Carol isn't staying. I'm sure she'd have something to say about that."

"Great Aunt Carol has something to say about *everything*."

Mom's phone rang, and she groaned when she looked at the screen. "It's the caterers. Now what?" She strode out of the room.

Mike snuck an arm around Jake's waist, and Jake took a step away from him. "She could come back at any minute," he whispered.

"Then let's sneak into the summerhouse. Marcus and Seb aren't there." Mike sighed. "I just want to hold you."

The plaintive edge to his voice mirrored the ache in Jake's heart. "I know. I want to hold you too. But at least we get to share a sofa bed tonight."

"Sure, in a house full of people," Mike said gloomily. "We'll need to behave."

"What you *really* mean is, we can't behave badly." Jake closed the gap between them, and kissed Mike lightly on the lips. "But tomorrow we'll be home." He retreated to a safe distance, acutely aware of his mom's presence.

This sucks. This really sucks.

"It's not home anymore." When Jake frowned, Mike smiled. "It's sanctuary. I looked it up. 'A place of refuge or rest. A place where you can feel at peace.'"

Yeah, sanctuary pretty much nailed it.

Jake put on his coat and went out the back door. Not that he needed a coat—it had to be in the high sixties out there. He walked toward the rear of the yard, where a path led into the trees.

"Escaping already?"

Jake started. Marcus stood at the door to the summerhouse. "Christ, Marcus. You almost gave me a heart attack."

"I was just wondering what you were doing out here, when all the fun is happening in there."

"Fun?" Jake shook his head. "I came out here for some peace and quiet." The house was bursting at the seams with relatives, and they all wanted to talk.

"Where's Mike?"

"Mom discovered she didn't have fifty candles for the cake, so she sent Mike to the store for more." Jake peered beyond Marcus to the summerhouse. "Where's Seb?"

"Taking a nap before the fun *really* starts."

Jake chuckled. "Yeah right. You wore him out, didn't you?" He inhaled deeply. "The air is so much better here than it is in Boston."

"Let's not discuss the climate, all right? Let's talk about you."

Jake smiled. "I told you in my text. I'm okay. Really. I'm in a better place than the last time we talked."

"Yeah. It was the place that interests me." Marcus strolled toward him. "I hear you and Mike are roommates."

"Mom told you, huh?"

Marcus snickered. "She told me, Lisa, Robert… Anyone would think she was glad to be rid of you." He paused. "She also said how happy you seemed with the arrangement. She thinks you and Mike are a good fit."

"It's new, but yeah, we get along."

Marcus leaned in. "In *and* out of bed?" Jake blinked, and Marcus's eyes twinkled. "You can't pull the wool over *my* eyes, kiddo. You've got this glow about you. Mike too, for that matter, so it doesn't take a mind reader to guess what's going on behind closed doors. And that's the way you want it to stay, right?"

His pulse quickened. "You… you said you wouldn't say a word."

"And I won't," Marcus assured him. "Neither will Seb. Especially now that we've seen you." He reached out and ruffled Jake's hair. "I'm glad everything worked out. Happy is a good look on you."

"They need to invent a new word, because happy doesn't cut it anymore." Jake was *so* far beyond happy.

"Hey, get it in gear, boys," Mom yelled from the back door. "They'll be here in half an hour." She stared at Marcus. "Where's the boy toy?"

Marcus cackled. "Oh, he'll love that. I'll go wake him up." Mom nodded and went back indoors.

"Who can sleep with your sister around?" Seb said in a sluggish voice. His usually unruly hair was worse than ever.

Marcus pointed to the summerhouse. "You might want to look in a mirror before you go into the house. Company, remember?"

Seb rolled his eyes. "Fine. I'll drag a brush through it. But it's *your* brush—I forgot mine." He retreated inside.

Marcus put his arm around Jake's shoulder. "I meant it when I said I'm happy for you two. I just wish everyone else could see how good you are for each other."

"And *I'm* happy no one else sees as well as you do," Jake confessed. The more he thought about it, the more he yearned for the weekend to be over. Being on his guard all the time was exhausting.

Sanctuary beckoned, and he couldn't wait to get back there.

Jake gave his grandmother a tight hug. "Is everyone forgiven now?"

She chuckled as he released her. "I kept telling your grandfather, I was going to disinherit the lot of you. I should have known your mom would do something like this." She glanced around, then whispered, "She's the sneaky one of the family." She beamed. "But when I walked into the living room, and you all shouted…" Grandmomma wiped her eyes. "It was a wonderful surprise."

"I'm glad."

She peered across the room to where Matt and Donna were talking animatedly with Matt's mom, Lisa. "Isn't it good news about Matt and Donna?"

"Great news." They'd announced their engagement during the buffet, to much applause. Jake had regarded their happy faces with mixed emotions.

They can share their *love.* He couldn't repress the wave of bitterness that washed through him.

"Are there going to be fireworks tonight?" Granddad asked as he joined them. "You know, carrying on the family tradition."

Jake smiled. "Mike and I set them up before you arrived. And seeing as we've eaten, and the sun set three hours ago, I think it's time, don't you?" Across the room, Mike nodded, and Jake raised his voice. "Everyone? We're going outside for a final check, so if you'd like to take your places either outside or by the windows, we should be ready to light up the sky in about five minutes." His announcement was greeted with applause. Jake kissed his grandmother's cheek. "See you when it's over." Then he followed Mike to the kitchen and out the back door.

Mike coughed as they walked across the patio and headed for the rear, his flashlight illuminating their path. "*We're* doing a final check? *We* should be ready? It's usually just me."

Jake chuckled. "Lord, you can be dense sometimes. Who's gonna see us out here? They'll all be watching the skies."

"That depends what you have in mind."

Jake waited until they were out of sight of the windows. "I just wanna kiss you without an audience, that's all."

"Aw." Mike sighed. "Yeah, I like the sound of that. But wait till I've lit the fuses, okay?" He aimed the flashlight at the fireworks, checking each one. "We're good to go." He lit the taper and when the tip glowed, he set off the first round, then hurried back to Jake.

Jake didn't look at the colorful display once. He only had eyes for Mike. They kissed, their arms around each other, hidden from the living room windows. Each new round of fireworks brought more kisses, and when Mike set off the finale, Jake poured his heart and soul into their kiss.

"I love you," he said as bursts of gold lit up the night sky above their heads.

"Love you, so much." Mike stroked his back.

"I still find it hard to believe this is happening. I keep thinking any second now, I'm going to wake up and find it's all been a dream."

"An amazing dream," Jake added. The last bang died away, and it was over. He sighed. "Oh well. Time to go back to reality."

They walked slowly toward the house, and as they stepped through the back door, applause broke out. All the guests crowded into the kitchen, and Jake was confronted by a sea of smiles. Robert had even pushed Great Aunt Carol into the room in her wheelchair.

"That was awesome!" Sarah said, beaming. "Dad said it was the best one yet."

"Everyone?" Mom raised her voice. "One more surprise left." All eyes turned toward her. "There's champagne for a toast. Marcus, you can help me pour."

Marcus tugged his hair. "Yes, ma'am." That got him a chorus of chuckles. "Do the kids get a sip?"

"A *tiny* sip," Ashley stressed. "That's if they come downstairs. They were watching from the attic window." She walked out of the room, and hollered for Alex and Sophia.

Mom went to the fridge and removed the champagne bottles, and Marcus tore off the foil and loosened the wire cages. He met Jake's gaze, his eyes twinkling. "Your mom is going to make me remove all the corks, because it scares her when they go *pop*."

"It does *not*," Mom remonstrated. "It's just

that… you're better at it than I am."

"Sure. We'll go with that." Marcus handed Seb a bottle. "Here. Make yourself useful."

It wasn't long before the corks were flying, and Mom and Marcus were filling the glasses standing on the countertop. Jake and Mike handed them out, and when everyone had a glass, Mom raised hers to his grandparents. "Mom, Dad… Congratulations on fifty years of marriage, and defying the Gilbert Curse." That earned her some chuckles. Everyone drank. Mom raised her glass once more. "And here's to toasting you at your Emerald and Diamond anniversaries."

Granddad pulled a face. "What—you mean I don't get time off for good behavior?" Grandmomma dug him in the ribs with her elbow, and he quickly kissed her on the cheek. "I think you're amazing. We made it to fifty years without me ending up under the patio. Because Lord knows, I can be trying."

She widened her eyes. "You think I'm going to argue with that?" Then she smiled as laughter erupted around them. She raised her glass. "To our wonderful family. May you be as lucky as I was, and find someone who completes you, makes you laugh—and puts up with all your foibles." Glasses clinked.

"Can I have some?" Sophia's clear voice rose. She emerged from the gathered relatives, Alex behind her.

Ashley smiled. "A little. Let me get you something to drink it from." Her gaze met Grandmomma's. "Something that isn't as fragile as your vintage glass." She went to a cabinet.

"Mom, why were Jake and Mike kissing?" Sophia said loudly. "Are they boyfriends now, like Uncle Marcus and Seb?"

Oh fuck. Jake froze to the spot.

Ashley frowned. "Of course they're not. Don't make up stories. I've told you about doing that." She gave Jake an apologetic glance. "Sorry. This is a recent thing. She's proving to have quite an imagination."

"But they *were* kissing," Sophia protested. "I saw them from the window in the attic. They were standing behind Great Granddad's shed when the fireworks were going off. Honest, Mom." She rolled her eyes. "I've seen Uncle Marcus kiss Seb lots of times. I *am* nine, you know."

Mom stared at Jake. "Sophia *is* making it up, isn't she?"

Jake swallowed, and beside him, Mike became a statue. "Mom… I can explain…"

In the silence that fell with a thud, Jake was aware of every pair of eyes focused on them.

Fuck.

Marcus Tells It Like It Is

Jake wasn't surprised the first volley came from Mike's dad.

"What do you mean? What's to explain? You're *cousins*, for Christ's sake. Mike, you'd better start talking."

Lisa gazed at them in horror. "You… you can't be serious. This is so… wrong." Her brother Robert wore a similar expression. Grandmomma gaped at them, Granddad too. Great Aunt Carol had her hand to her chest, her mouth open, her brow so furrowed her eyes almost disappeared from sight.

Jake turned to Mike. "You know what? I'm not gonna stay around to be roasted. You with me?" Mike nodded, his face a mask of misery.

"You're going nowhere, not until we know what's going on." Uncle Chris's face was flushed.

"But you *already* know," Jake protested. "Sophia just told you. Yes, we were kissing. Why? Because we're in love with each other. So now you're all shocked and disgusted, we're gonna leave. Don't worry. We won't turn up at any more family gatherings." He grabbed Mike's hand and pushed through the assembled muttering relatives, his heart pounding, heading for anywhere but there.

I should've known.

"Wait!" Marcus's voice rang out, loud and clear. "Stop right there."

Jake came to a halt, his legs trembling, his chest heaving.

Marcus pointed to the living room. "Everyone, in there. Now." He glanced at Alex. "Take your sister and go play in the attic for a while, all right? Can you do that for me?"

He nodded, then took Sophia's hand. "Come on, you. I have a puzzle to work on. You can help me find the edge pieces."

When the kids were out of earshot, Marcus glared at his relatives who were still standing in the kitchen. "Did you all go deaf suddenly? Go sit down."

One by one, grumbling, everyone put their glasses down and filed out of the kitchen, until only Marcus, Seb, Jake, and Mike were left.

Seb gave Jake a huge hug. "Hey, we've got your back, all right?"

"I'm glad someone does," Jake murmured. When Seb released him, Jake glanced at Mike. "Well, it's not as if we didn't expect this."

Marcus squeezed Jake's shoulder. "You knew it had to come out one day, right?"

"Sure, but not this soon. And not like this." The disgust in Uncle Chris's voice…

"Okay. I'll do what I can to help, but you need to trust me. I'm on your side, remember?"

Jake nodded, and Mike's hand tightened

around his. "I trust Uncle Marcus. Let's hear what he has to say. Maybe he can help."

Jake doubted it, but they had nothing to lose. "Okay."

Marcus stared at the door. "Here we go. Damage control time." He led the way into the living room, where every available seat was taken. Sarah, Matt, Ashley, and Donna were on floor cushions, and the remaining adults were on the couches and armchairs. Great Aunt Carol was in her wheelchair, her lips pressed together. Everyone fell silent as they entered, and it only served to exacerbate Jake's roiling stomach.

Marcus pointed to the rug in front of the fire. "Jake, Mike, you sit there." He waited until they sat cross legged before gazing at the room. Seb stood at Marcus's side.

"Did you know about this?" Mom demanded.

Marcus nodded. "Jake told me how he felt two weeks ago. And I'll be honest, I reacted like most of you. A fact I'm not proud of. Because if I'd taken a moment to think, I'd have seen there is nothing wrong with the love these two share."

"Nothing wro—" Uncle Chris glared at him. "They are first cousins, for Christ's sake."

"And?" Marcus stared back at him.

"What do you mean, *and*? There are laws about this kind of thing."

"I don't see what the problem is," Sarah

muttered. When all eyes turned to her, she frowned. "What's the big deal? So they're cousins. So what? What's wrong with that?"

Marcus gave her a grateful smile. "Exactly." He glanced at Matt. "What do *you* think?"

Matt shrugged. "To be honest, I'm with Sarah. I can't see why everyone's making such a big deal out of it. Why is it anyone's business if Jake and Mike are in love?"

"That's because you're young," Great Aunt Carol declared, her voice quavering. "You haven't seen what I've seen. Children born with terrible physical and mental illnesses, all because their parents were first cousins."

Sarah blinked. "But what does that have to do with Jake and Mike? It's not as if one of them is going to be pregnant, right?"

Marcus beamed. "Precisely. Now, before I present the most glaringly obvious argument why Jake and Mike have nothing to be ashamed of, let me go back to what Aunt Carol said." He gazed at his relatives. "What I'm hearing in this room from the older generation is a gut reaction. It's ingrained in us, and no wonder. Ever since Jake told me how he felt about Mike, I've been reading up on the subject. I learned that marriage between first cousins is illegal in thirty states, whereas if these two lived in Europe, no one would bat an eye. Hell, in parts of the Middle East, Africa, and Asia, such marriage is considered preferable. Not that anyone is talking marriage at this point," he added quickly.

Jake's face heated, and a tide of red rose up Mike's neck to stain his cheeks.

"And about those birth defects," Marcus continued. "Yes, there's a slight risk, but so slight that most physicians today would argue such laws should be abolished."

"Damn it, this is incest," Robert insisted.

"Dad, that's a little strong, isn't it?" Josh retorted. Sarah and Matt murmured in agreement.

Marcus gave Robert such a hard stare that Jake quaked to see it. "Incest is between siblings, or parents and children. It is definitely *not* the case here. And frankly, for an intelligent man, I'm surprised at you." Robert flinched. Marcus addressed the room. "Sarah nailed it. At least *someone* in this family has some common sense. All these laws… *None* of it applies when it comes to same-sex relationships." He sighed. "Look, I know how easy it is to say something in the heat of the moment before you've had a chance to think. I was the same, okay? But if you just took a minute or two to reflect, you'd realize that what taints your view of this situation is the stigma." He pointed to Jake. "I wish you could've seen the turmoil I witnessed, when Jake finally revealed his feelings. He's loved Mike for so long, and what stopped him from *telling* Mike, from confessing that love?" Marcus glared. "Exactly the crap some of you spewed out a few moments ago."

"Uncle Marcus is right," Sarah announced.

"Has no one in this family ever heard the phrase Love is Love?"

"I don't think they have trouble with Jake and Mike being gay," Matt muttered. "Their problem lies with them loving each other. But I agree. Uncle Marcus makes a lot of sense."

Silence fell once more, but Jake couldn't help noticing the burning cheeks, the way some of his older relatives crumpled in their seats, the chins that dropped to chests, the hitch in their breathing…

Mom cleared her throat. "Now I know why you've taken up writing," she murmured. "You have a way with words." Her gaze met Jake's. "I'm sorry. I didn't think."

Jake swallowed. "It's okay." Jesus, he was shaking.

"No, it really isn't." Mom shivered. "Marcus is right. None of the stuff we've grown up believing applies to you two. Hey, maybe it doesn't apply to anyone anymore."

"I don't think we can say that," Robert said. "We don't have all the facts."

"Well, we do when it comes to these two," Mom fired back. "Unless you think one of them is about to miraculously grow a uterus?" Robert gave her an abashed glance.

Mike looked at his dad. "Are we good?"

Uncle Chris's Adam's apple bobbed sharply. "I flew off the handle, didn't I? Marcus was right. All I could think of was what people would say. Sarah's right too, and Matt, and Josh. We're all making such a big deal out of it when it really isn't." Another swallow. "So yes, we're good. And if it's not too late to say it… I'm happy for you. When I think back on the way you two have been your whole lives… it all makes sense. Maybe you were meant to be together."

Judging by Great Aunt Carol's cough, not everyone in the room was in agreement, but Jake didn't expect them all to fall in line with Marcus's thinking.

"Is there any champagne left?" Seb piped up.

Mom chuckled. "There's a lot of champagne left. Why?"

"Because maybe we need to drink another toast." Seb's face glowed. "To Matt and Donna's engagement, and to Jake and Mike finding each other."

The gleam in Marcus's eyes and his high chin spoke of his pride.

"I think that's a wonderful idea." Grandmomma's voice cracked. Mom got up from the couch and hurried into the kitchen.

Jake stood and went over to Marcus and Seb, Mike close behind him. Jake threw his arms around his uncle, and held him tightly. "Thank you," he whispered.

Marcus kissed his cheek. "Hey, we rainbow sheep need to stick together, right?"

Jake hugged Seb. "All the time Marcus was talking… I think that was the quietest I've ever seen you."

Seb rolled his eyes. "You have *no* idea. But I couldn't say a word. It had to come from Marcus. This isn't my family."

"Do you really think that?" Granddad came over to them. He patted Seb's arm. "Did no one tell you?" His eyes twinkled. "We adopted you this summer. Welcome to the Gilberts." He turned to Jake and Mike. "Ignore everything Jess says about the Gilbert Curse. I have a feeling you two will work out just fine." Jake stared at him, and Granddad arched his eyebrows. "You don't agree?"

"Oh, I agree all right. It's just that… well… I didn't expect *you* would. Especially after what Great Aunt Carol said."

Granddad smiled. "Ah. I get it. You thought I'd be… what's the phrase… *freaked out* by your revelation?" Jake nodded. "You're too young to remember your grandmother's cousin, David. Nice boy. Lived with a sweet girl called Holly. His *cousin* Holly. Everyone thought they shared a house out of convenience, but your grandmother and I, we knew the truth. And no, it wasn't something we shared with my sister. Carol has always been old-fashioned when it comes to things like that." He patted them both on the arm. "I think you two will be very happy together."

Mike shuddered out a sigh. "I think you're right." And before Jake could agree, Mike took him in his arms and kissed him. A couple of *aws* broke out, followed by a smattering of applause.

When Mike released him, Jake gazed at him in surprise. "Wow. When you come out, you *really* come out."

Mike's smile was beautiful to behold. "No need to hide how we feel anymore. No more secrets." He squeezed Jake's hand. "Not everyone has our backs—I don't think either of us ever expected that—but enough of them to mean family gatherings are still a go."

Jake was glad about that.

Robert walked up to them. "Look… this is difficult, okay? Marcus presented a very logical argument, but… I'm finding it hard to overcome my emotional response with logic. So bear with me, please. I'm sure I'll come around eventually, but it might take a while." He flushed. "And I'm sorry I said what you share is incest. That was wrong." He glanced at Marcus. "These two are lucky to have you in their corner, because I don't think anyone else could have dealt with the aftermath of Sophia's bombshell the way you did. It had to come from you." He held out his hand, and they shook. Robert cleared his throat. "And now I think I'll take Mom to her hotel. I don't think she should stick around here."

Jake had a feeling he was right. "Thank you for being honest."

Robert smiled. "You're welcome." Then he walked away.

Marcus patted Jake on the back. "Once I find a place, you and Mike will be welcome to come stay with us." Seb nodded in agreement.

"Thanks." Warmth radiated through Jake, and his heartbeat raced. He squeezed Mike's hand. "You know what? I think it's going to be all right."

Mike kissed him on the lips. "All because you found the courage to tell me how you felt."

Jake shook his head. "No. This is all because I followed Seb's advice." He smiled. "I followed my heart."

The End

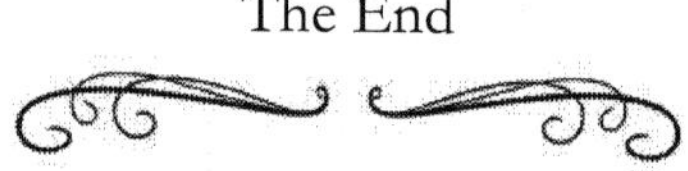

ALSO BY K.C. WELLS

<u>Learning to Love</u>
Michael & Sean
Evan & Daniel
Josh & Chris
Final Exam

<u>Sensual Bonds</u>
A Bond of Three
A Bond of Truth

<u>Merrychurch Mysteries</u>
Truth Will Out
Roots of Evil
A Novel Murder

<u>Love, Unexpected</u>
Debt
Burden

<u>Dreamspun Desires</u>
The Senator's Secret
Out of the Shadows
My Fair Brady
Under the Covers

<u>Lions & Tigers & Bears</u>
A Growl, a Roar, and a Purr
A Snarl, a Splash, and a Shock

Love Lessons Learned
First

Waiting for You
Step by Step
Bromantically Yours
BFF

<u>Collars & Cuffs</u>
An Unlocked Heart
Trusting Thomas
Someone to Keep Me (K.C. Wells & Parker Williams)
A Dance with Domination
Damian's Discipline (K.C. Wells & Parker Williams)
Make Me Soar
Dom of Ages (K.C. Wells & Parker Williams)
Endings and Beginnings (K.C. Wells & Parker Williams)

<u>Secrets – with Parker Williams</u>
Before You Break
An Unlocked Mind
Threepeat
On the Same Page

<u>Personal</u>
Making it Personal
Personal Changes
More than Personal
Personal Secrets
Strictly Personal
Personal Challenges
Personal – The complete series

Confetti, Cake & Confessions
(FREE)

<u>Christmas</u>
Connections
Saving Jason
A Christmas Promise
The Law of Miracles
My Christmas Spirit
A Guy for Christmas
Dear Santa
Santa's Secrets
Christmas Lights & Sleepless Nights

<u>Island Tales</u>
Waiting for a Prince
September's Tide
Submitting to the Darkness
Island Tales Vol 1 (Books #1 & #2)

<u>Lightning Tales</u>
Teach Me
Trust Me
See Me
Love Me

<u>A Material World</u>
Lace
Satin
Silk
Denim

<u>Southern Boys</u>
Truth & Betrayal

Pride & Protection
Desire & Denial
The Southern Boys Trilogy

Maine Men
Finn's Fantasy
Ben's Boss
Seb's Summer
Dylan's Dilemma
Shaun's Salvation
Aaron's Awakening
Levi's Love
Maine Men – the Complete Series

Salvation
Wrangled
Haunted

Second Sight
In His Sights
In Plain Sight
Out of Sight

CrossBow Protection (with Parker Williams)
Broken Warrior
Broken Wheels

Standalones
Kel's Keeper
Here For You
Sexting The Boss
Gay on a Train
Sunshine & Shadows
Double or Nothing

Back from the Edge
Switching it up
Out for You (FREE)
State of Mind (FREE)
No More Waiting (FREE)
Watch and Learn
My Best Friend's Brother
Princely Submission
Bears in the Woods
Holy Hell – with Parker Williams
Teasing Tim
Str8 B8
Taylor-Made for Me

Anthologies

<u>Fifty Gays of Shade</u>
Winning Will's Heart

<u>Come, Play</u>
Watch and Learn

<u>Writing as Tantalus</u>
Damon & Pete: Playing with Fire

ABOUT THE AUTHOR

K.C. Wells lives on an island off the south coast of the UK, surrounded by natural beauty. She writes about men who love men, and can't even contemplate a life that doesn't include writing.

The rainbow rose tattoo on her back with the words 'Love is Love' and 'Love Wins' is her way of hoisting a flag. She plans to be writing about men in love - be it sweet or slow, hot or kinky - for a long while to come.

Made in the USA
Middletown, DE
08 August 2024

58758397R00085